QUICKSILVER

Daphne,
Thanks so much for your
attentive reading, wonderful feedback
and gentle yet fearless presence.
You've been a wonderful mentor, as
well as a role model.

Nadine
Banff, 2005

QUICKSILVER

stories by

Nadine McInnis

Nadine McInnis

RAINCOAST BOOKS
Vancouver

Raincoast Books acknowledges the ongoing support of The Canada Counc.l; the British Columbia Ministry of Small Business, Tourism and Culture through the BC Arts Council; and the Government of Canada through the Book Publishing Industry Development Program (BPIDP).

First published in 2001 by
Raincoast Books
9050 Shaughnessy Street
Vancouver, B.C.
v6p 6E5
www.raincoast.com

Edited by Joy Gugeler
Cover photo by Robert McCann / Photonica
Cover design by Val Speidel
Author Photo: Gordon King

1 2 3 4 5 6 7 8 9 10

CANADIAN CATALOGUING IN PUBLICATION DATA
National Library of Canada Cataloguing in Publication Data

McInnis, Nadine, 1957-
    Quicksilver

    ISBN 1-55192-482-X

    I. Title.
PS8575.I54Q52 200! C813'.54   C2001-910851-6
PR9199.3.M3175Q52 2001

At Raincoast Books we are committed to protecting the environment and to the responsible use of natural resources. We are acting on this commitment by working with suppliers and printers to phase out our use of paper produced from ancient forests — this book is one step towards that goal. It is printed on 100% ancient-forest-free paper (100% post-consumer recycled), processed chlorine- and acid-free, and supplied by New Leaf Paper; it is printed with vegetable-based inks by Friesens. For further information, visit our website at www.raincoast.com. We are working with Markets Initiative (www.oldgrowthfree.com) on this project.

Printed and bound in Canada

For Tim

CONTENTS

SEA MONKEYS

It was hard to believe they were measuring out life with a miniature plastic scoop, freeze-dried or held in suspension indefinitely, until they added water. The directions made it sound as simple as that: *Add water and a few small scoops of magic sea monkey food, store in a stable warm place and watch the cavorting begin.* But he had to tell Alexander that it wouldn't be a real circus of monkeys like the cartoon drawing on the envelope, that there wouldn't be hand-to-hand spins on the trapeze.

Alexander peered into the canister of water. The small eggs swirled to the bottom.

"They won't grow very big," he warned his son as they cleared a spot on the kitchen counter for the sea monkey canister. "There's not enough heat and light in here."

"When will they come to life? Will they have fur?"

"They're not really monkeys. They're little shrimp, but not the kind people eat."

His wife looked at him and whispered, "Tell him they'll be fun."

"Fun?" he asked her, alarmed for a moment. He still felt the shock of seeing the small foil envelope of sea monkeys lying on the hall table with the other opened mail: square, festooned with colour, advertising pleasure. He thought someone had sent his wife a condom. But taking a closer look at her, he couldn't imagine who would have. She was pale and fine-boned, with a straight mouth on a sharp jaw that contradicted her gentleness. He towered a foot over her with dark disorderly hair, a middle starting to soften.

"He's been waiting for two months for this to come in the mail. Tell him it's worth it," she said softly, having moved up close to him.

"It's worth it," he said to her.

She smiled at him and he felt the echo, a faint tickle tugging the corners of his mouth. It was a reflex stored deep in the nerve endings that had strengthened during the years of their marriage. His response to her was automatic, habitual, but not deeply felt.

With the other woman, it was the opposite. Every time he caught her eye, he felt like a diver, disoriented. His past and future were murky, and he had told her this, knowing that she wouldn't misunderstand.

The other woman asked him if he had felt this way before, perhaps when he had met his wife.

"The opposite. She rescued me," he told her. "She fixed my photos of Greece after they had been destroyed in a flood. Once they were fixed, I thought I didn't need them or even poetry anymore. And that's the story of how I became a drone."

He had laughed ruefully. She studied him with her shadowy eyes. Although she was young, her eyes had the weary cast of middle age.

"I can't imagine you've given up. The poems must still be in you. Humming." She put her dark head against his chest and they stood like this for several minutes. He thought of the pale, pitted statues of Greece, the way they had reflected his male beauty when he was too young to know they would outlast him. The warmth of her head emanated through his shirt to his skin, reminding him of the strong sun as he had lain on a stone slab at the Temple of Poseidon overlooking the Aegean. Byron's name was still carved into one of the pillars but he had been unable to find it. He lifted her face, kissed her and said, "You almost make me believe it's still possible."

"Almost. I didn't think there was anything 'almost' about this. Should I check to see if my hymen is still intact?"

She surprised him, as she always did, and he laughed.

"Did you know that I slept at every major archeological site in Greece? History puts me in a horizontal position."

She laughed in return. "I'm not that old."

"But you're an old soul," he said, touching the pointed tip of her nose with his mouth. "I would hide until the tourists left, then settle in. The clear Greek light woke me early. It's true what they say about the quality of light there. I wrote and wrote, leaning on a toppled Greek god for a few quiet hours before the guards came and kicked me out."

"Bring me one," she said. "I want to read a poem by you."

He drew away from her then, moved behind his desk and locked the right drawer with a key he kept in his pocket, a signal that their conversation would soon end.

"They're all gone."

He was embarrassed now by the old-fashioned brown ink carefully scribed in unlined notebooks. A flood in his father's basement had destroyed them. A summer storm backed up the sewers and erased his careful artifice and all his heady self-important words. He had peeled apart each sodden page, amazed. They were all blank, as though he had never written anything at all.

"So, how did she fix them?"

He looked at her, puzzled.

"Your wife. How did she fix your photographs?"

He told her about the photography store where he brought the damaged photographs still glued together with sludge and melted chemicals. And even though he knew she was a summer student, was only the one to take the wrecked package from his hands and deliver it to someone else, he associated their miraculous recovery with her intervention. He had flipped through the crisp, square photos, explaining each to her in detail.

"In the damage still evident around the edges, I could almost see a Greek chorus forming, the swirling shape of togas, small sarcastic gods pointing at me on the Aegean, at Knossos, me smiling as though I would always be the centre of the universe. I knew it wasn't true anymore. So I got married and started my PhD."

He and the other woman spoke to each other this way, in stark revelations, as though his dim office at the university was a confessional, as though they could say these things he would never want another person on earth to hear, and walk back to their lives absolved.

"What is her name?" the woman asked. "You always call her 'my wife.' That's so sexist."

"Catherine."

"Catherine," she said, considering. "As in Catherine and Heathcliff?"

"No. As in Cathy."

"Cathy and Bruce. The perfect suburban couple. I bet you have big showy flowers in your yard. All white."

He knew there wouldn't be a message waiting for him. Not yet. Not before midnight. Checking his e-mail was the last thing he did before going to bed, even when Cathy was still awake. She would kiss him on the cheek and let him go. His study was sacrosanct, her way of acknowledging the dreams of being a writer he had given up for her. Every night, as the young woman's words swam up, glittering, to the surface of his screen, he thought, I should be sleeping by now, I should be dreaming, but he needed very little sleep these days.

"I imagine you in a glass house, wide expanses of glass, light pouring in," she had written to him in the beginning, when this imagined self seemed more real than his daily self, even to him.

And when she grew bolder, she wrote, "Your eyes are icy and airless. I look at you, so radiant."

How that had thrilled him, like a shock at the base of his spine.

She was a visual arts student, but despite her metaphors of light, she was full of gothic shadow: lipstick, eyeliner and hair too dark for her pale face. He imagined the two of them intertwined in a sinuous vine of blood, equally passionate, perfectly matched. She dressed in the colours of an old priest, royal purple and black, an occasional shocking flash of white.

When he came away from her and walked through the front door into his house, these thoughts subsided. The generous glass of the dining room was a theme carried throughout. Light slanted in from the golf course late into the evening. Their house was built at the end of a fairway, near the twelfth hole.

"Who would put all this lovely glass in the line of fire?" Cathy had asked when they were considering the place. But not one ball had sailed even as far as the hydrangea that marked the boundary of their property, laden now with heavy white blooms.

He stood at the window, looking out across the green. A yellow flag moved, almost imperceptibly, toward him. Someone was carrying it a short distance toward a hole. *Like Birnam Wood coming to Dunsinane Hill.* MacDuff's soldiers held tree limbs before them, a forest advancing toward the castle. He made a mental note to tell the young woman this.

Like the lengthening days, he too felt filled with light. Everything in his world seemed to shine, the cutlery in his hand, the cut glass salad bowl, the matching gold rings on their fingers. He helped Cathy with the dishes, bantering, snapping her with the towel as he stood behind her at the sink. He put his arms around her as darkness rose from the fairway, making their reflections suddenly distinct in the window. She had changed so little from the day he met her. In the glass, the fine wrinkles beside her eyes were not visible. Her body against his was lithe, her buttocks firm against his stirring groin. She reached out and lifted the plastic container of sea monkey eggs from the windowsill.

"The nights are still a bit cool, and Alexander's heart is set on this," she said. "Where should I put them?"

He slid his hand under her shirt and cupped her breast.

"Just swallow them. It worked before."

She laughed. "I'm done with all that. Besides, you know I don't swallow."

"I can always dream."

"You can always beg."

They went to bed early. Alexander was ushered to the bathroom to brush his teeth and then to his own bed, the comforter covered with moons and stars pulled up to his chin.

He opened a space in the slats of the blind as he waited in their bedroom. The moon rose full over the apple tree in the front yard. The blossoms were past their prime, their white edged with curling brown, but the radiant petals caught the slight breeze and blew the scent through the screen. He was thinking of her standing before him naked, the small tattoo of the moon circled by stars just below one

7

of her heavy breasts, the nipple a deep red, raised from the darkness of the aureole.

In bed, he rolled Cathy over, her pale curls wavering in slow motion like underwater fronds. Cathy beneath him, the other woman above, enveloping, salty, her long-fingered hands smelling of sex. Even in class, when he walked by her, he caught a whiff of it.

He let go and caught Cathy's hand, swinging it high above her head, holding her down. She lifted her chin and groaned. He felt the mouth of the other woman on the back of his neck. They turned again, hand to hand, counter-clockwise on the bed. Quickly the women interchanged, a pale nipple, then a dark one in his mouth, the hips both fine-boned and heavy drawing him in, across the bed now, his feet and legs dangling out over empty space, not even he could say which one he was thinking of when he came.

Within three days, the sea monkeys had hatched. He sat with Alexander at the breakfast table. Each morning since they had watched the eggs fall through the water, they had measured out magic sea monkey food with a small scoop. He suspected all it contained was salt, dissolving without a trace. The water was clear and still. Even with a magnifying glass, they had been unable to see anything until today. And suddenly there they were, little blond specks of life, transparent, almost invisible legs whirling and propelling them up and down through the water.

"They're alive! They've alive!" Alexander cried, jumping with the canister in his hand.

"Careful, you'll spill them out before they've even had a chance to grow. Cathy, come here and take a look at this."

She leaned over the table, smiling faintly as she gazed at the water, then leaned over and kissed Alexander enthusiastically on the forehead.

"Well, you did it. Congratulations. You'll make a fine father."

By the time Alexander came home from school, there were more than a hundred swimming specks. He watched, enraptured, until bedtime.

After Alexander was asleep, they agreed this was better than television. Why hadn't they discovered it earlier?
"But what do we do if they keep hatching? We start with a pinch of nothing and all of a sudden we've got Calcutta on our hands," she said.

"Don't worry," he said. "We won't tell Alexander, but I think brine shrimp are cannibals. Only the strongest survive."

Sometimes, after his night class, he walked her to the market district where she lived with a roommate. They never turned onto her street. Neither of them had seen where the other lived. It was a neighbourhood of stylish shops, old rooming houses and slow circling traffic, brilliant at this time of year with outdoor vendors' colourful produce, flowers and bedding plants. He imagined she had small herbs in planters on her windowsill. She would snip them in the morning, releasing strong aromatic mists in her run-down kitchen: spearmint, rosemary, lemongrass.

He knew it would not be one of those trendy renovated buildings, but rather one with a flat roof, long, thin, dirty windows and a fire escape. The windowless bathroom would have pressed tin squares painted black nailed to the ceiling, a transom over the door. He could see her lying in lukewarm water in the claw-footed bathtub with light from the hallway lapping as she shifted her leg. He could hear the glassy splash as she lifted her hand and admired the curve of her forearm.

The moon, still full, but beginning to narrow, rose above them as they walked slowly from the university. She had wanted to stay in his office as they usually did, but this time when he saw her standing in the doorway, a button undone below her throat revealing the pale skin of her chest, he felt unaccountably tired.

"I was at the studio," she said. She stepped into the room and he smelled again the salty sexual smell of her, the strong smell of her dark hair.

"I saw your light on." She pointed to the small window. His office had once been a bedroom in a private home; now it housed the English department. The bricks, windowsills, front porch had all been painted a dismal grey. The house still had its original Victorian layout: hallways that led to dead ends, shallow useless coal-burning fireplaces in all the rooms. The wooden floors under the carpet creaked with ghosts. The bathroom outside his office was actually two small rooms, one containing a deep, stained bathtub and sink, the other, only a toilet. These traces of prudery had been an aphrodisiac. When she had first come to his office, the light behind him lit up her pale skin, careless black hair and the sharp lines she drew under her almond eyes. She could have been a young woman corseted, with an older cruel woman standing behind her, placing her foot on her spine and tugging, pulling the laces tight. He could imagine the winces, the hissing sound her mouth would make with each sharp tug, the same sound she eventually made when he first entered her. Nothing was as necessary as this pain. People, as well as time, could be superimposed. On an impulse, he told her this.

"Imagine the people who slept in this room. Did they know it would be a public place one day?"

"Imagine the people who *didn't* sleep in this room," she replied, so certain he would respond.

He stepped from behind his desk and stood before her, doing up the top button of her shirt. It was a fatherly gesture. She shrank back. He moved toward her again, put his arms around her and placed his chin on top of her head. She responded, reluctantly, by putting her arms around his waist. The posture still felt fatherly so he drew away.

"You're here late. What have you been doing?"

"I'm working on my fossil exhibit. The bones are so brittle. They're always breaking before I get them in place. I'll never be finished."

He was surprised, realizing that they hadn't talked about her work, only his own.

"Fossils of what?"

"Right now, a fossil of a toaster." She grinned at him, interrupting the intensity that drew him to her.

"I take`fish bones and lay them in clay, the shapes of contemporary domestic household objects. The cutlery fossil was fun, so was the electric beater, but toasters lack mystery, I guess."

She had registered that he was putting papers in his briefcase.

"I get my bones from a seafood restaurant in the market. Why don't you walk with me?"

Then he knew that what surrounded her was not the smell of sex, but of art, her own particular, painstaking art. The fingers she had held to his face stirred something so deep within him that he had assumed it was chemical.

She led him through the residential streets, away from the strip of brightly lit restaurants. The moon faded in and out. Under the lights on the corner, it barely existed above them. Then it strengthened until it was humming overhead, caught in the wires.

Here the prostitutes and addicts were bent over, nursing a powerful pain, or standing, pelvises cocked, thighs outturned, hands on their hips.

"The moon draws them out," he said. "Like the coral."

"What?"

He had hoped she would ask. When he read about these things, he saved them, anticipating the pleasure of telling her. Instead of writing the poems he might have written when he was her age, he spent the images promiscuously.

"Somewhere in the South Pacific, all the coral breed on

the same night. During a full moon in spring. The waves are filled with red eggs and milky sperm carried out on the tide. I've always thought people need that. One night when they can do whatever they want, for the sake of social order."

She didn't respond as she usually did, picking up the thread, spurring him on.

"One night?" she asked, although it wasn't meant to be a question.

They came to the corner of Sussex Drive. She took his arm and pulled him across the street to the National Gallery. It rose before them, a majestic building made almost entirely of glass. Inside the tallest tower a massive red scarf was pulled and mounted in a lovely fluid swirl.

She led him down wide concrete stairs toward a Greek-style agora, a pit ringed with seating where, in summer, jazz bands played to the lunch-hour crowd. The stone benches were blue under the moonlight. Despite the lack of audience, the pit was far from empty; it was packed with small makeshift roofs, angles of corrugated sheet metal, little passageways, hasty sheds.

"Is it under construction?" he asked her.

"No. This is an art installation. It's a barrio, but it's under guard now because the homeless tried to move in. I love the irony of that. Would that be life imitating art or art imitating life?"

Beyond the red silky rope and the sign, NO ADMITTANCE AFTER HOURS, he saw the twisting alleyway leading between the shanties, the quickly constructed boxes of scrap wood and sheet metal. The moonlight made deep pleats of shadow on ridged roofs. His heart quickened when they ducked under the rope, no guard in sight, and meandered through the exhibit, walking single file when a corridor was particularly narrow. He would have trouble finding his way out without her. He felt as though they were moving inwards toward the centre, although the moon over their heads held its position.

She stopped and turned to him, placed her open mouth against his and her body blossomed outward, her breasts pressed against his chest. She eased him through a low doorway. He bumped his head before stooping and stepping backward into the dark room. They were beyond seeing then, beyond hands, mouths. He was impatient with the cool skin of her thighs. She had once called her body her 'meat dress,' making fun of an art exhibit that had inspired a month of angry letters in the local paper. He wanted to take that off, too, her flesh flayed and red with want, and get to something more enveloping than her body. He would remember something important, something about himself that had been lost.

He pressed her against the inside wall, his fly open now. No condom. The slippery source touched and shifted away from him as the wall gave and creaked behind her head. She almost lost her balance, but he found his way inside her, stabilized her against the flimsy wall. He wouldn't have heard the moan, would have thought it was coming from her, from him, from the air, if she had not frozen, a sudden clenching inside her, surprisingly unpleasant.

"Someone is here," she said.

He moved again, sending himself into her, hoping to catch again her dark silty depths. She pushed him back. The air was cold and he felt his arousal slipping away. She moved away from him and ducked under his arm. He leaned his forehead against the wall, the sweetish smell of vomit close at hand.

He heard her voice in the dark below him.

"It's a man. He's sick."

"You mean drunk."

"I don't know. Can't you hear his breathing? It's rough, like there's something caught in his throat."

"Drunks always snore. All I smell is vomit. Let's get out of here."

"No. He's sick. I'll stay here and make sure he keeps breathing. You go find the guard. Get help — fast!"

"He's crawled in here to sleep it off. Just let him be."

"It's more than that. Can't you see?"

"I can't see much of anything," he said and laughed. She didn't respond. "I can't be here, you know. How will I explain it?"

"Just tell them you washed in with the coral. For the sake of social order." She was angry. "Go then. I'll take the rap. Just send the guard."

He had hoped he would find the guard, point in the right direction and be done with it, but he lost his way. He finally saw the red rope arcing between two brass poles. Traffic passed in a steady stream, but how could he justify stopping cars for a nonevent like a homeless man sleeping off a binge in this neighbourhood of bars and night carousing?

When he got home, he paused before going through the front door. His wife had hung a thick industrial chain from the eaves where the corners of the roof met. In the winter, this chain prevented the buildup of ice, so instead of a dangerous icicle, a beautiful silver rope shimmered from roof to ground. This was one of the things he loved about her: the way she surrounded them with practical beauty, the way the beauty she created was so safe. He held the chain, wet with dew. He could hear the frogs singing in the pools of the golf course, an endless shree, as though they never needed to draw a breath.

His family was asleep. He went first to Alexander's room, moving through the dark, to sit on the side of his bed. The stars and moons of the comforter glowed yellow-green, even where they peeked out from the fold of his son's sleeping arm. Alexander's bedroom was at the back of the house, and all he could hear was the joyous promiscuous frogs making the most of a beautiful spring night. He leaned over to kiss Alexander's forehead, anticipating the warm smooth brow even before his lips touched, but was surprised instead to feel ridges of plastic against his mouth. He felt with his hands, puzzled. Alexander had fallen asleep with his swimming goggles on. He had missed taking him to his lesson tonight. Turning the light on, he saw his son's eyes tightly closed, magnified slits behind plastic. Fetal, sightless, swimming through the night.

He sat that way for a long time, looking down at his son. He didn't remove the goggles. In the morning he would have red rings around his eyes like a raccoon but he would have seen things coming through the blurred darkness that could save him in later years.

In the middle of the night, he heard the phone ring downstairs, angry, accusatory. It brought him immediately to his feet. He got there as the answering machine clicked on. As he reached across the counter to erase the trace of her angry sigh, he felt lukewarm water soak his pants from groin to knee. The canister of sea monkeys was tipped on its side. Minuscule crustaceans were clinging to his pyjama bottoms. The phone had fallen off the hook and a fast, panicky busy signal pulsed from the receiver. His wife came sleepily into the kitchen as he was mopping the floor with the dishcloth, wringing water into the canister. Only an inch or two of cloudy water had been saved. She didn't notice what he was doing.

"Who called? Has something happened?"

"No, love. No one. Just dead air. Why don't you go back to bed? I'll be there in a minute."

She smiled, reached up with one hand as though discovering her ear for the first time, and turned back toward the hall.

Even with the canister up to the light, no little windmill arms were visible. He peered through the magnifying glass that came with the sea monkey kit. Nothing but shreds of debris drifting on small invisible whirlpools. He didn't want to face Alexander in the morning. How could he explain his carelessness? He carried the canister to the sink and filled it with clear, cold water, set it back on the counter. Life so transparent, it could have disappeared into thin air. Perhaps it was never really there at all.

He knew a message was waiting for him. And like so many other nights, instead of heading for bed, he slipped into his chair and turned on the computer. There was her name written in dark heavy letters next to the time: 3:17 a.m. But there would be nothing thrilling in her note. He knew what she would have to say. He moved the mouse and clicked the delete button. Emphatic words spring up: YOU ARE ABOUT TO DELETE AN UNREAD MESSAGE. ARE YOU SURE? He didn't want a second chance. He erased her completely, every word she had ever sent. For a moment, he was tempted to open several of his own messages to her, to read who he had been before this moment. He was still convinced that he had given the best of himself to her, but the small pinch of grief in his chest passed. Message by message, he deleted his own fervent words and watched his screen fill up with empty, still water.

QUICKSILVER

Ally has learned to adapt the way she reads her poems to suit the deviously imaginative modes of interruption each town offers. A spitfire delivery to compete with the basketball game and shrill whistles coming from the gymnasium, a jerky alternating rhythm in the room next to the bowling alley. "All things long," she says, waiting for the inevitable crash before adding, "for demolition."

Lately she almost believes she is as desolate and lonely as poetry in the modern world. It's easy enough when she hears her voice repeating certain lines, "such delicate silence, insulation pushed into place," in rooms with only a handful of women in the audience, dressed carefully and made up for this rare night out in a small town. More than once, an old-fashioned black phone starts to ring on a desk in the room, and rings and rings like a summons from some dark muse. She pauses mid breath, mid line, waiting, until one of the lipsticked women jumps up and answers, says in a soft querulous voice, "No, he's not here. No one's here right now." This makes her pause and wonder if it's true.

But the cities are worse. The lonely, the wounded, the narcissistic, read their own poems before she rises as the featured guest. Every city seems to have women whose skulls shining beneath the overhead light are more articulate about chemotherapy than their poems could ever be.

She takes her seat again after reading in Regina and a man sitting behind her leans forward and says, "Beautiful poems."

"Thank you," she replies, about to turn toward him fully when he says, "Your hair has been hanging over the back of the chair and I've been playing with it. It's beautiful, too," and she stops and pulls her hair over one shoulder to shelter her quickly beating heart.

What Morgan had warned her about is true. "Why don't you tie it up? You attract weirdos with that hair," Morgan said as they stood in line for a foreign film at a decrepit repertory house more than twenty years ago. Morgan was a restless elderly woman swaying from too much booze, even then. But at the time, Ally was starstruck.

Ally's hair was less of an enticement for danger that night than the vacant lot where Morgan had insisted they park, next to the Bell Hotel on Main Street. It was a part of Winnipeg where white people rarely ventured, especially two white women at night. A green neon bell was lifted by an invisible hand, ringing over and over on the narrow vertical sign. Morgan's face shone with a hectic, green on-again off-again intensity. "Never send to know for whom the bell tolls; it tolls for thee," Morgan had said, laughing.

"Hemingway?" Ally asked.

"John Donne," she answered. "You young poets think nothing was written before 1900."

She had felt that familiar blend of gratitude and humiliation. Morgan acknowledging her as a poet. Morgan reminding her how little she knew.

The summer she spent as Morgan's secretary was her first experience of poetry alive in the world. Before that, it had been a private tunnel that let her slip in and out of the suburbs where she was raised. In a new city full of wind, Winnipeg's animate air, she was convinced that life could be as intensely structured and heightened as the poetry she loved best.

She had met Morgan when she was a first-year student at the University of Toronto. She had brought poems to her as the writer-in-residence. Morgan had a reputation for telling students they should go into law or business if she disliked their writing. But with Ally, she had been gentle. She showed her how to use line breaks to enhance emotional tone, untangled her adolescent syntax, convincing her she didn't have to say everything in one poem, but could let the reader discover just one true perception.

When the term was over, she asked Ally to come to her office to help her pack her books for her return to Winnipeg. Ally waited on the doorstep outside locked doors on a grey, dripping Sunday afternoon in April. When rain began to fall in earnest, she walked to Morgan's campus residence. The students had left the week before for hometowns and summer jobs. On the fourteenth floor, the elevator doors slid open, giving her a view of a grey head, face turned away, lying on the floor. She rushed over to Morgan, relieved she was still breathing. In fact, she seemed to be snoring. Her open purse lay on its side, change, lipstick, pens, a couple of pill bottles, a pocket notebook and a small Swiss Army knife on the floor beside her. The knife was clean, blade open.

Ally touched Morgan's neck to feel for a pulse and Morgan stirred, pushing her hand away, saying in a tired voice, "Help me up." Ally managed to lift her to a sitting position, but she could not lift her to her feet. Morgan clawed awkwardly at her coat, locked in the closed door of her room. Then everything came together: the cloying sweet smell, the dumped purse, the ability to fall asleep on cold linoleum.

"Where are your keys?" she asked.

Morgan gestured at her door in disgust, a slow sweep of her hand.

"I'll be right back," Ally said, heading off to find the custodian.

Once they were safely inside Morgan's room, the master key returned, the dangerous blade of the knife folded back into itself, purse refilled and snapped shut, Morgan sobered up and stood moodily at the window speckled with rain.

"I hate rain," Morgan said by way of explanation. "April *is* the cruelest month …"

Ally smiled, delighted to be able to reply, "Breeding lilacs out of the dead land."

"Mixing memory and desire," she sighed, indicating that this wasn't a game. "Stirring dull roots with spring rain."

"You must be lonely here. You're still far from home."

The lines " miles to go before I sleep / and promises to keep" occurred to her but she didn't say them out loud.

Frost was too far removed from the elegance of Eliot. She didn't want Morgan to think she had pedestrian tastes. Morgan turned from the window and smiled at her, a beautiful, sustained smile that lit up the gloomy room.

Now, more than twenty years later, Ally is the poet Morgan wished her to be, still trailing behind her the waist-length hair that Morgan had hated. She starts to take an inventory of Morgan's influence. She now says "yes" instead of "yeah," isn't reticent about sexual content in her poems, lives with cockroaches in her kitchen in the name of virtuous poverty, has made a small name for herself as a feminist writer. She would prefer to live without the cockroaches, but they seem to go with the territory, words scuttling from crumb to crumb, all the poems she's written harbouring a life of their own, furtive, excited by light, determined to breed.

On the negative side, she has not changed her first name to something daring and androgynous, Starling or Lee. (Morgan insisted that Ally was no name for a poet, but thought her given name, Alyssum, was even worse). She has married the man Morgan dismissed. She still favours a gentle, lyrical realism. And another thought she can't bear to admit. She's begun to lose poetry, her bright words, like the shiny cutlery Morgan spilled onto the floor when drunk.

Morgan wrote under the influence of cheap white wine. Ally shadowed her, made sure she didn't leave the stove on or lock herself into the stairwell, retrieved forks, spoons and knives when Morgan stumbled or pulled kitchen drawers out too far, and most importantly, transcribed her wild scrawls the next morning. This was the bright birth of poetry, these quicksilver flashes and threats of fire. But even for Morgan, after the joyous Dionysian creation, came the long, dark night. She sat inert on a kitchen chair, her chin sinking lower onto her chest, slurred retorts directed at her dead husband and father who, she told Ally when sober, had wanted her to fit their idea of a woman, had tried to silence her. Ally retreated, left her to find her own way to bed. The sounds of Winnipeg at night, the racing motor-cycles, sirens, the drunken brawls a block away on Portage, gave Ally the texture of her own dark poems written in perfect sobriety.

Morgan surprised her one night by placing her hand on her shoulder in the dim living room of her small apartment in one of the older, rougher areas of Winnipeg. Ally had been sitting at a makeshift desk constructed out of a door and filing cabinets, meant to last only the summer. She hadn't noticed Morgan reading over her shoulder. Hadn't noticed, either, the voices of two little girls singing in the stairwell. It was midnight and a bad neighbourhood, but here, unmistakably, were girls' voices singing in circles, winding down, then laughing together on each intake of breath, delighted by their own echoes.

"I had to see if you were writing about them," Morgan said. "Before I could." She bent closer and Ally could smell wine, although she seemed sober.

"You could remove that second "the" and streamline the image, make the verb active. It's good, Alice, but watch the abstraction." She let the misnomer go because Morgan's suggestions freed and simplified her lines. She made the corrections, then turned to see Morgan sitting in a wing-back chair much too formal for her living room.

"They remind me of my sister and me. We were so close. As you grow older, you also grow more isolated." They listened to the girls singing outside the door. "Aging would be too grim without poetry." After a quiet moment, she said, "She had a good death."

"Your sister?" Ally asked.

"Yes. In an Irish forest. She was walking her dogs, a vessel burst in her brain and it was over. The way it should be. Her dogs were off their leash. She was a talented painter, you know. But only a Sunday painter. Too many family responsibilities."

They wrote quietly side by side late into the night. Two women's bodies, sweating lightly, bright and metallic, pitched to catch every fleeting thought, memory, syllable. Morgan was the first person she had ever experienced this kind of connection with. If anything marked the beginning of her commitment to poetry, it was that night. She can still measure a poem's potential by the smell of her own body. That strange mineral smell meant that the poem plumbed deeper than her own experience; it tapped bedrock, underground rivers.

She had looked for the same kind of connection from her mother the night that poetry, coiled tight behind mere words, leaped off the page and seized her when she was thirteen. Ally had carried the anthology down the stairs, the page open to words Sappho had written thousands of years before, yet as potent as they were when the ink was wet.

With his venom

Irresistible
and bittersweet

the loosener
of limbs, Love

reptile-like
strikes me down

Her mother seemed embarrassed as Ally sat stricken beside her, the irresistible and bittersweet words inside her from then on.

When the windows started to lighten, Morgan's daylight efficiency started to kick in. It was the space between drunken inspiration and sleepy despair that Ally dreaded the most. Then Morgan turned her desire to renovate the world full force on whatever was at hand.

"Don't do it," she told her. "You'll never write."

Ally felt herself blushing, knowing instinctively what Morgan was talking about.

"Stephen doesn't want a servant."

"Don't believe it. I have yet to meet a man who is willing to boil an egg. Let me tell you what married love is like for a writer. I was in London after the war, visiting my sister, when the call came about my husband. It was sudden, a

heart attack. I went out and walked the streets all afternoon. The buildings were blasted to bits. Bedrooms with
old rose wallpaper hanging open in the sun and rain. Layers
of roses shredded and flapping in the breeze. I kept thinking of all the women who had counted those roses doing
their duty, hearing a voice in my head saying over and over,
'I'm free. I'm free.'"

"People don't wallpaper their bedrooms anymore."

"Just go down a few layers. You'll find it. As far as men
are concerned, women are good for two things: counting
roses on the wallpaper, as quietly as possible, and carrying
water jugs on their heads."

"But you never left your marriage," Ally said, hearing
her own voice tense and defensive.

"I had to write. How could I afford to do what I was put
on earth to do? They were different times."

"No need to earn a living, no children. Sounds pretty
free to me," Ally said, angry then. The summer was coming
to an end, frequently unraveling into mutual irritation.

As it turned out, Morgan had been wrong. Ally's husband,
Stephen, loved the poet in her, and she had kept her hair long
for him. He lay beneath her, happily drowning in her hair, or
above her, smoothing the dark length of it over her breasts.
She wondered if such romanticism balanced his days at the
paper plant along the Ottawa River, coordinating shipments
to central Canada. Although she didn't go there often, it was
a place more surreal than any place she could dream up in
her poetry. The factory was a throwback to harsher industrial
times; the grey stone walls cobbled together, small, dirty
squares of leaded glass, an all-male world full of racket, a

prison. Outside, the river itself was a maze of sluiceways and dams that harnessed the power of what had once been rapids and waterfalls.

"What else do you do with an arts degree? Good benefits. I'm not complaining. You know I never had any great ambitions. I'm content," Stephen said to her when she asked him if he wanted more. He was happy to see her at the end of the day, her old jeans torn at the knees, her hair unbrushed, dishes piled in the sink because it meant she had been working happily, lost to the world. A different kind of chaos met him when the children were babies. She had been impatient then with a day spent snatching an hour here and there for reading or writing when they were asleep. Then, she needed to place a baby in his arms and head straight out the door to walk by the river. Lately she has been wondering what his days must have been like if he could arrive home to her distraction with such enthusiasm.

Tomorrow, for the first time in twenty years, she will return to Winnipeg for a reading and appearance on a local TV talk show, then home to Ottawa to finish her tour by reading with Morgan, probably for the last time. Morgan, now in her late eighties, has grown frail, suffers from mild forget-fulness. She wrote to Ally from one of the Gulf Islands, where she'd moved when Winnipeg's winters grew too harsh for her brittle bones, to ask her to arrange a reading.

Actually, someone named Beverly had written the let-ter, saying that Morgan was eager to see the Emily Carr exhibit at the National Gallery and would Ally also arrange for a private tour before the crowds pressed in. It was an eerie letter because the voice was so clearly Morgan's, but the third person point of view, handwriting and signature belonged to a stranger. She was amazed at Morgan's arrogance, but even more amazed when the curator offered to escort her through the exhibit himself.

The talk show guests are unnaturally quiet, now and then casting glances at the monitors bolted high in the corners of the room. All that is being televised at the moment is a turquoise couch and matching high-backed chair, occasionally the backside of a technician taping down a cord, shifting lights. The televised furniture glows with a strange expectancy. In the corner, a large white rabbit sits propped in a chair. Assuming it is stuffed, her eyes skip over it. Then its head suddenly swivels, turning its plastic aqua eyes toward her.

She recoils and starts to count her breaths. On the monitors, the producer is counting backward, ten, nine, eight, seven ... Her counting and his meet at the number six, which calms her. When she opens her eyes, she sees a young man watching her, still a rabbit from the neck down. His eyes are watchful, his skull shaved, an edgy urban style. He holds the rabbit head on his lap and speaks directly to her.

"We're running late today," he says, as if warning her.

"I must have been dreaming. Almost everyone is gone," she says.

Then the producer enters again and summons the last man, who turns out to be the mayor of a small town north of Winnipeg made famous when a migrating whooping crane dropped dead and fell onto the football field.

The rabbit tells her this story without a sense of irony.

"What kind of a show is this?" she asks.

"Oddities, local happenings."

"Oddities," she repeats.

After a moment more of silence, the rabbit asks her, "What are you in for?"

"Poetry," she answers. "What about you?"

"Charity. I end the show every day by raising money."

"Is the show almost over?" she asks, suddenly alarmed. He lifts an enormous white paw, bites the end of it and eases it off, revealing a pale, long-fingered hand, strong as a pianist's. She sees that he's looking at his watch.

"They've run out of time," she says.

"I think so," he says before pulling his paw back into position and lifting the rabbit head from his lap.

After the show is over, her makeup is removed. She has expressed, holding her anger tight in her jaw, that she will not wait for a chance to appear on the following day's show. She stands on the street in front of the station feeling exhausted by stress hormones. She thinks of calling the promotional person at her small literary press and sounding off, but decides there is no point.

She recognizes the grey stone Anglican church across the street. It is squat, ugly, has a yard gone to weed. The curving flower beds are filled now with tough stems tied in knots by the wind. One of the leaded windows narrowing to a point like a teardrop has been boarded over.

This is the church she drove by once, when Morgan shrieked, "Stop!"

"What's wrong?" she cried, putting her foot on the brake.

"Those flowers," Morgan had said. "I want to dig up those hollyhocks for my uncle's grave."

The church's gardens were beautifully tended then, someone's labour of love, but Morgan could not be dissuaded. Her uncle had loved hollyhocks, and here they were. She fell to her knees and plunged her hands into the earth. The pale hem of Morgan's beautiful Irish linen skirt was covered with dirt. Ally eased her back and finished the job herself as Morgan paced excitedly above her. She lifted the flowers, with their roots and as much soil as possible, into a plastic bag they had found in the trunk. No one stopped them. This certainty was at the heart of Morgan's poems, too: a willingness to get her hands dirty, rearrange colour, root one thought in the rich soil of another.

They replanted the hollyhocks at the graveyard several blocks away, this time with a trowel they stopped to buy at Canadian Tire.

"You shouldn't have to scratch at anyone's grave with your bare hands, dear. You're too young for that," Morgan said, laughing at their audacity.

The grave had been dug midwinter and by late summer had started to heave a little, as though its tenant was resting uneasy and wanted out.

"He still isn't content to stay put," Morgan said, suddenly pensive. "I held his hand in the hospital all through that last night. And do you know what he said? 'I don't want to die. I don't want to die.' Ninety-three years old, deaf, unable to walk and he didn't want to die."

"And what is so intricate, so entangling as death? Who ever got out of a winding sheet?" she answered.

"You've been studying." Morgan bent down to touch the silky petals of the hollyhock. Then she reached out, impulsively, and stroked Ally's hair. "John Donne. My favourite."

She starts to walk the four blocks to the graveyard, curious to know if their handiwork is still in evidence, but she hears her full name, Alyssum, called softly behind her. She turns to see a young man dressed in a black shirt and jeans walking toward her. He has a shyly expectant look on his face. He is slender and it takes a moment for her to realize where she has seen him before.

"You know my name," she says to the young man who had worn the rabbit suit.

"I read your book when it came in. It was very, very fine." It is an oddly formal phrase from someone so young. He takes it from his back pocket. A little shudder passes through her when she sees that her book has been rolled like a newspaper, the rich purples and bright stars of its cover, the universe of her inner life, carried like spare change.

He riffles through the pages, then stops, drawing his fine-boned muscular hand to the title, "Amnesia," a poem that describes the evaporation of a pond until nothing is left but a dry bowl of cracked dirt. She found just the right plant life, the tiny swimmers in the pond's depths: manna grasses, water lettuce, the hollow spherical colonies of the volvox, somersaulting hydra, the ephemera of dragonfly nymphs, sinuous ribbons of leech, the tiny fairy shrimp. The shrimp, that swim on their backs and mate with their lengths pressed together, the male's claspers gently holding the female and their multiple leaf-like arms caressing the surface of each other's bodies. She wanted the pond to be rendered in such vivid detail that it would not be a metaphor, but a tragedy in its own right.

"This one," he stops, speechless. "This one." He doesn't finish his thought but puts his closed fist to his chest.

She feels dark water rising, held back momentarily in her throat, then spilling from her eyes.

"Hey," he says, and she feels his hand on her shoulder. "It's a good thing. Whatever it takes, just write more of them."

The night they are to read together at a small art gallery in downtown Ottawa, Morgan calls her from the hotel and tells her to read for only ten minutes. Morgan knows it will be good for Ally's career to read with someone of her stature, but she must realize that at eighty-seven, Morgan needs an early night. She can hear from the slurred belligerence of her voice that Morgan has been drinking.

Ally is surprised by how frail Morgan has become. She stands in the lobby, leaning unevenly on a cane too tall for her, thin to the point of emaciation, her white hair grown fine and long, pinned up in a French roll. Ally catches sight of her scalp, bluish-white beneath the baby-fine tendrils. In old age, she has regained the ethereal look she had in photographs taken in the 1920s, the long forearms and femurs, the astute grey eyes challenging the camera. When Ally is close enough to see her clearly, she discovers that her eyes have turned blue, giving her pale face less calculation and more empathy. She's wearing one of her long silk dresses, pastel, joyous, flowing from the sharp bones of her hips. Here is the Morgan that audiences love, all grace and celebration. Whatever she heard on the phone must have been the understandable crankiness of the very old, or her own sensitivity. She gives her a quick hug. Morgan moves her face aside and as Ally is withdrawing, she sees Morgan pushing away a few of Ally's long dark hairs from her electrically charged silk shoulder.

"I've held out," she tells Morgan. "And you've come over to my side. Your hair looks wonderful long."

Morgan responds by taking a step backward, stumbling slightly. When Ally reaches out to steady her, Morgan glares.

"You almost pushed me over."

"I didn't," she answers, injured.

Morgan gestures to her books on the couch. Ally picks them up and guides her to the car outside the glass doors.

"I don't know why you're reading tonight. It will only disappoint people who've come to hear me."

"The gallery thought it would be nice."

Morgan laughs, a quick exhalation. "I hope you're writing intelligible poems now. You used to be so obscure."

Ally can't help herself. She has to ask, "Do you mean you haven't read my books? I sent them to you."

"They're publishing so much these days. Many young women have been influenced by my work. How could any of you know what it was like for women back then, how much we struggled for every chance to be heard and read."

Ally pulls the car over to the side of the road, puts the gear in park. It has started to rain; the windows have misted up.

"I asked you a question."

"What, dear?" Morgan asks mildly.

"Did you read the books I sent you?"

"Of course," Morgan says, turning toward the window, content to watch the traffic lights spray red and green drops against the glass.

Both women are quiet the rest of the way to the gallery. Morgan nods off several times, but stirs and smiles when Ally opens the door for her at the gallery.

"Did you make sure this was well publicized?"

"The venue would have handled that."

"Was it in the newspaper? I've had many students over the years."

"I saw it in the Saturday paper and the CBC announced it."

"Did you call them, to arrange an interview while I'm here?"

"No," she says, and instead of apologizing, she fishes for their books and her own clipboard of unpublished poems from the dark back seat of the car.

She is starting to feel the familiar dread of standing before an audience. This pattern precedes her readings: intense apprehension followed by mild despair. She knows she must find the bathroom soon or she will be unable to get through it. She sees several of her writer friends, but she holds back, returns their waves across the room.

Morgan has transformed herself into the beneficent matriarch surrounded by a circle of women. One takes Morgan's books, another takes her hand and loops it through her arm to take the place of the cane. Morgan is lowered into a chair and immediately, a semicircle of women leans towards her and settles around her.

Ally realizes she has lost her own books when she is being introduced and must climb over Morgan's legs to check the washroom. She enters again the cramped room, the stalls painted a deep blood red, the ceiling and walls a flat black without shine. She's disoriented, starts to shake when she doesn't see her books and papers on the counter. The sinks are empty silver bowls, scooped, surgical, quivering with a queer, wan light. She bangs open one stall, then the next, spots her clipboard on the floor. Her new poems are here, one page slipping out with half a shoeprint tattooed over the first three stanzas, but there is no sign of her books. Size five or six, she thinks. The small, furtive feet of a thief.

The door opens, letting in a warm rush of air. She hears her name, and her friend, Nicole, tentatively pushes open the stall door and finds her sitting, fully clothed, on the toilet.

"Are you sick?" Nicole asks. "Or just panic-stricken?"

"My books are gone, my reading copies," she says, discovering she is close to tears.

"They can't have gone far. I'll check around the back.

Ask the audience if anyone accidentally picked them up."

"Some accident. Whoever took them left my new poems here on the floor."

"The ultimate compliment! Poems worthy of a felony."

Laughter, for just a moment, starts to win out. She wants to sustain it, to continue sitting here mesmerized by the tiny mirrors embroidered into Nicole's dress.

A request from the front of the room does not yield her books. She stands before the audience, a few sheets of paper shaking in her hands, and tries to concentrate on reading, but her eyes are drawn to all the feet in the room, looking for the smallest, daintiest shoes. She hears her voice as a delayed reaction. The words live in her mind and her throat and then later bounce hollow against the hardness of the audience. It's like a long distance phone call from the other side of the world. Then there is the sudden cascading jingle of silver hitting the hardwood floor. She looks up and sees that Morgan has her wallet open. A few coins are clinging to her lap. For a moment, the shininess, the cool silver flowing off Morgan's lap, strikes her as beautiful. She waits for the commotion to subside as the women around Morgan scramble off their chairs to pick up change, but she knows her reading is truly over, that Morgan's lovely laughter will carry her up here to the podium. She has read for exactly six minutes.

The next afternoon, on his way back to work after a meal break, Stephen drops her off at the glass doors of the hotel where she is to meet Morgan and take her by taxi to see the Emily Carr exhibit at the National Gallery. In the car, he leans toward her to say goodbye, not quite meeting her eyes. He touches her hand, touches her face when she delays stepping out, her hand on the door handle, telling her she doesn't have to be here if she doesn't want to be. She turns toward him, smiling at her good luck, to be with such a man.

In the hotel room, Morgan seems overjoyed to see her. She takes one of her hands in her own and surprises Ally by quoting lines from her truncated reading the night before:

Cocoons hang above their off-season shoes.
Their hands, more papery by the year,
reach within the depths of filmy light,
waiting for touch to catch fire again.

"Such a wonderful poem about marriage, that lovely image of the wedding dress as a cocoon," Morgan says. "But of course it isn't about you two. You're one of the great success stories."

The slight tremble in the corner of her mouth suggests wistfulness, although it is more likely the strained nervous system of the elderly.

"Please, sit here beside me," Morgan says, lowering herself onto the bed. "I've written a poem. First time in so long. I woke up from a dream about your cocoons. Your poem has been sounding inside me all night and this one answered."

She starts to read in a hushed, spellbinding voice:

A woman cannot withdraw, although
there is a place folded quiet and still
nestled within her broad lap, an origami bird.
A woman's body is not paper though it can burn
like paper, a bright chemical flare lighting two faces
before leaving her charred with its residue.

Ally realizes she hasn't taken a breath since Morgan began. She looks down to the page's pale blue ink, Morgan's quick, sharp handwriting, like lightning. Her hands are sinewy, pale as skim milk, the fine bones hollowing, and they are shaking slightly so that the paper seems to be quivering of its own accord.

A woman opens, the waters part,
tunnel walls are translucent, swimming with life.
He is a fiery thread passing through
the eye of the storm safely, choosing
the moment to lie drying on the far shore.

Morgan's voice trembles with emotion, she pauses, then continues:

A woman waits for emptiness before she can
close again, the waves ease and the surface heals
but sometimes that tug is too abrupt, she is tossed
alone, and his body releases a sluice of sadness
that washes through her ...

Ally feels the emotion of the poem aching inside her

and loses her concentration for a few moments. The next lines propel her beyond the metaphor and certain phrases ring clear. *Echoing her inner shape, a hook cast out clean and easy.* She watches Morgan's hands put the poem aside and return to her demure, dry lap. Where does such pain come from, she wonders, and this from a woman who claimed no man could be more important than poetry. From memory, the gift and curse of all writers, she thinks.

"Morgan, thank you. It's not yours. It belongs to the world."

"Perfect praise for a writer, and true. My guardian angel gives me a poem, but the trickster usually takes it away before I can get it down," Morgan says. "Old age can be cruel. You know what Emily Carr wrote about it? 'Old age is lonely and bitter when taken sip by sip, to the dregs.'"

"Are you lonely, Morgan? You have so many people who care for you, care about your work. I know, I used to answer all those letters."

"The only company I ever really cared about was the company of my poems and they are few and far between now. I don't know what I'm doing here if there are no more poems. I don't want to outlive them. I want them to outlive me."

"They will."

"They could be just so many scraps swept away. Nothing like what you have with your children."

"I'm more than a broodmare, Morgan," Ally says.

"I know that, dear. You have both, children and poems. You were very wise."

After a time of sitting companionably side by side, Morgan says, "You must keep on, Alyssum. Promise me you will." She is surprised that Morgan has used the name she was given; this is the evidence she was looking for that Morgan has read her books.

"I hope so."

"You're right. Hope is the best we have."

They hear a low, far-off droning, like the approach of bees, then the traffic sounds on the street outside the hotel organize into the even beat of a drum and the high notes of a pipe band. Ally rises and looks out the window at Elgin Street ten floors below.

"You should see this, Morgan. It's the changing of the guard heading for Parliament Hill. We won't be able to leave until they pass by." Below them the tunics are perfectly symmetrical, a red rectangle of dots marked by the tall bearskin hats, moving at an even, unhurried pace, stopping traffic in both directions.

They both hold the sheer curtains back and lean forward until their foreheads are touching glass. The crowd lines the street with the bright, random colours of summer clothes. They mill about chaotically, hemming in the logical, ceremonial pattern created by the foot guards. Morgan laughs, "Rather compulsive, isn't it? That's what we're up against. And don't ever forget it."

Later at the National Gallery, the crowds will come for the opening of the exhibit; there will be speeches, white wine, glistening trays of strawberries and red grapes, but for now there are only Emily Carr's paintings and these airy, empty rooms. The curator has given them a brief orientation before being called away. Ally is haunted by the missing years, 1914 to 1927, when Emily didn't paint, so discouraged was she by the lack of critical interest in her work. At forty-one, the age Ally is now, she must have thought her creative life was over. The paintings before this silence are lovely enough. They are quiet, impressionistic, with a light palette, but Ally thinks they feel studied, cautious, maybe even dishonest in their desperate need not to be criticized.

They stand before *Indian Church*, with its narrow white building, its delicate white cross dwarfed by a swirl of thick green vegetation, jungly, growing so high it blocks the sky. Here is Emily, finding her vision and her courage, well into her fifties. The lush rainforest flows like water, flame and muscle, throbbing greens, delicate folded flesh with such potential for stretching and strength.

"She's so sexual, even more than Georgia O'Keefe," she tells Morgan.

"O'Keefe was consciously sexual, but Emily was a prude. It has to go somewhere and here it is for all of us to see," Morgan says.

They move on to a swirl of cerulean sky at dusk, flecked with yellow, spiralling above the tops of thick evergreens. She leans in to read the title: *Above the Trees*, 1939.

"This is the painting she was working on the time I visited her studio," Morgan says.

"You knew her? Really?"

"Not exactly. I met her once. A professor at Victoria College, Ruth Humphrey, brought me to meet her, writer to writer. Emily was working on her books then, and she was painting this in her studio that day. She had chairs tied up on ropes near the ceiling. If she wanted you to stay, she lowered them on a pulley. She lowered only one chair that afternoon, for Ruth." Morgan pauses, smiling at the painting, before adding, "She was a vulgar, vicious woman with a monkey on her back. Woe was the monkey's name. Or was it Woo?"

"It was Woo. Her last painting was of Woo."

"Well, it should have been Woe, like the rest of us. Life is mostly pain. Writing or painting takes you further into the heart of it."

"Then why do it?"

"Because if you do not turn toward life, you might as well be dead."

Ally says what she has barely been able to articulate to herself. "I'm losing faith, Morgan."

"That happens."

"But never to you."

"It gets harder to write as you age. With the first book, you're so thrilled to see your words in print. The second book consolidates everything you've tried to achieve in the first. You see what you've been able to learn. With the third, things get a little more uncertain. Is there growth or stagnation? You're not sure. Perhaps you're not a sweet young thing anymore and the male reviewers decide you're old hat. The fourth is a struggle. You're pushing stones up a hill. But it's what you do and it goes on from there. You hurt the way a dancer always hurts."

She can hear the fatigue in Morgan's voice. Ally suggests that Morgan sit in the Great Hall until the speeches begin that will open the exhibit and finds her a chair close to the podium so that when the time comes, she'll be able to hear. Then she returns to face Emily Carr alone. The painting she stands before is called *Scorned as Timber, Beloved of the Sky*, painted when Emily was sixty-five. A long, wispy trunk rises like a thin flume of smoke into a pulsing steel-grey sky. It is a ridiculously skinny junk tree left behind by loggers. The tree is crested by a tiny yet joyous cone of green life.

It reminds her of a red bandana being passed hand to hand during the reading she gave in a small town in Saskatchewan, improbably called Livelong. Reaching down to steady herself as she began to read a poem called "Savouring," she accidently put her hand in the oily well of a typewriter. Even before she had reached the end of the page, a man near the back had untied the red bandana from around his head and passed it up through the small audience for her to wipe the ink off. It was still warm from his head and from the hands of everyone who had touched it, a lovely flash of red joining everyone in the room.

She hears a low drum, a heartbeat rhythm, slow and processional. There are women around her now dressed in long, black dresses and dramatic silver jewelry, men with thin ponytails gelled back, looking as sleek as otters. Her friend, Nicole, meets up with her at the balcony overlooking the crowds in the Great Hall who are configuring into circles, then reconfiguring, kissing each other's cheeks, swirling into ever-changing constellations. It is dark outside and the spectacular floor-to-ceiling windows let in the lights of Parliament Hill, the dark expanse of the river traversed by a steady line of headlights moving across the bridge.

"Did you ever find your books?" Nicole asks.

"No. I keep wondering if Morgan set it up."

Nicole laughs. Nicole is a painter, fair-skinned and cheerful, the pleasure she finds in her art a source of some envy for Ally these days.

"One of her devotees could have been shadowing me, just waiting for the opportunity to present itself," Ally continues.

"That's pretty sinister."

"I know, I know. I'm just kidding. Where would we be without gallows humour?"

"Raking it in. Academia. I've always wanted to drive a milk truck. What about you?"

"'To Bedlam and part way back,' as Anne Sexton said."

"That's true, too. Crazy or competitive. Take your pick. Still, nothing brings out the best in her like another writer's catastrophe."

"She was brilliant, wasn't she?" Ally says with some admiration.

"The dropped change certainly was ingenious. Talk about getting your way."

"I meant her poems."

"So did I."

They look down at the crowd. People smiling, greeting each other, gesturing with their hands as they speak. It is a holiday atmosphere, so different from the quiet concentration it takes to create the paintings they all have gathered to celebrate.

"How many of those people have chosen what they do?" Ally says. "I met a man in Winnipeg who wears a rabbit suit to work. And when I think of where Stephen spends his days, the racket alone would send me to Bedlam faster than poems ever could."

"Maybe work is a small part of his life. And when do you feel most alive?"

She realizes that this is not a question she has ever needed to ask herself, despite her doubts. She scans the crowd, trying to catch sight of Morgan. The drums have increased in tempo and volume, other percussive tones have been added. A modern dance company has started to perform, but instead of dancing on a stage, they are moving through the crowd, attuned to pattern, inventing the choreography as they go. Both the men and women dancers are dressed in crimson shifts, torn into rags, faces painted dead white. They stare ahead, trancelike, while executing remarkable challenges to gravity. A woman slowly walks up the banister of the marble ramp to the Great Hall.

The crowd parts and follows the movement of the dancers, a swirling knot of people around each one. The dancers' vivid red rags contrast the sophisticated black of the audience. The woman who walked the length of the hall on the banister is now scaling a marble wall across from where Ally and Nicole stand. Although she is propelled only by her own strength, she strikes airy poses as she rises, seemingly weightless. The crowd has followed her and now Ally can see Morgan, alone in the area near the fruit tables and microphones. She sits marooned, her white head bent down to her chest, her large hands open, palms up, on her lap. She is asleep.

Suddenly a female dancer runs to the railing immediately beside Ally, then turns, and with a graceful exhalation, sweeps her hands in an arc on the floor. The angle of her wrists conveys passionate longing. Ally can smell the powder in her ballet shoes, see the drops of sweat on her plaster-white face, breasts rising and falling rapidly within her rag dress, her exertions invisible to the audience below. She knows the effort it takes to lend herself to this. The dancer turns again and Ally feels the crimson cloth brush against her leg, sending a shock wave up her spine. She will follow to see what comes next, a bright speck carried along in the dancers' wake.

THE LOTUS-EATER

I try to avoid looking at my reflection in the bus window: a woman holding flowers being ferried across a river. All day I've been going over poetry in my head, figuring out what I will read to him tonight in the hospital, discarding the *carpe diem* poems as too sexually charged, all those seductive arguments I'm long past now. *Gather ye rosebuds while ye may.* But I'm not carrying roses. Not the thousand female folds of carnations. I chose fern and one lifting bird of paradise. I'll have to keep the flower under wraps when I get home. Allen isn't going with me, and he might think it's too theatrical.

I hold his wife's hand in the hospital corridor. The dingy November light must never leave these halls. This was once a Catholic hospital for births and recoveries, but now it is just for the dying of all faiths or of no faith. When I passed through the doorway embedded in tons of grey stone walls, I saw myself stepping through a small hole at the base of a tombstone, some scurrying scrap of life, furtive and temporary, disrupting nothing much in the larger scheme of things.

Jocelyn, or Joss, as I've heard him call her, is a ghastly grey, twenty pounds lighter than she was in her aqua bathing suit at last summer's parties. More than one stone. That sounds right, given what she's going through. Even her hand feels less substantial than mine, cold-tipped fingers that twitch slightly against my palm. I let her hand go and she looks quickly away, toward the floor.

There's a whiff of cheap perfume that couldn't possibly be emanating from her at a time like this. Vaguely religious, and then I identify it. I used to think this was the smell of a blessing, the difference between holy water and ordinary water, before I learned that they perfume the fonts in churches. A small stone font in the shape of a shell leans out from the wall like a stagnant water fountain and is, surprising in these secular times, full to the brim. A faint coating of dust lines the water's surface, like skin. Not too many people dip their hands these days. Or perhaps too many do, sullying the blessing, here where church and hospital are blurred. The ceilings are so high you almost expect to look up and see clouds, the narrow recessed windows of leaded glass along the hospital corridor are peaked into sharp points, like steeples.

She surprises me by telling me, as though we've been intimate all our lives, "Just a few days more. I can't believe it. How can he go so fast?" and turns away again. Her sandy hair falls, hiding her face and she gasps as if coming up for air. She lifts her chin and looks me in the eye, a liquid gaze, almost sensuous in its misery.

"Jocelyn," I say, suddenly shaken. "Can I do anything for you?" It occurs to me that I should embrace her, but my hands are full — the flower, which suddenly seems too assertive or playful, the books in my arms.

"Joss," I repeat, softly, the way I've heard him say it, and she responds with a shudder. Her skin is stretched tight over her cheekbones, over suddenly sharp bones. I can barely see the heavyset woman he mysteriously chose and married, maternal in a way women no longer are, with a short waist, mild dreamy face. She's talking about endurance, the way these women always have.

"When I'm in there, I have to be strong. At home, I have to be strong. In front of my Grade 8 class, I have to be strong. I have the distance down this hallway to be weak. Sorry you had to be here for it."

"My God, don't apologize. Do you have any help with the kids?" I'm embarrassed I haven't thought of this before. I've sent Erica over with casseroles and desserts, white dishes of elaborate foods: kidney beans and artichoke hearts with mint, lady-finger custard cakes, squash sweetened with slices of peaches and a glaze of honey. Allen has enjoyed this sudden industry in the kitchen.

"My mother is on her way. She'll arrive tomorrow morning at eleven-thirty." She says this as though she's counting the minutes.

"Let me take the children tonight. They can sleep over and I'll bring them to school. Maybe you need a breather." Unbidden, I see his son and my daughter playing cat's cradle, their innocent hands brushing as they pass complicated patterns between them.

She starts to cry anew and I wonder if it's my words, the mention of breathing to a woman whose husband is dying of lung cancer.

"Thank you for coming to sit with him," is all she replies. "I don't want him to be alone, but the children are having a rough time. I have to leave now." She walks away, bumping into the wall before slipping out of sight.

I set the bird of paradise on the table beside his bed. A watery pattern wavers high up on the wall. The light is so subdued, he could be lying under water, so quiet, we could both be under water. A transparent mask is over his mouth, as though he is scuba diving. He opens his eyes without registering me. I glance down at my white sweater and realize that I must look like a nurse.

"Will, I brought you flowers, or *a* flower, I should say. One," I stammer and he focuses on my face.

"Oh ..." he says, almost a moan behind the mask, then silence. I think he's trying to place me.

"Gwen. It's your neighbour, Gwen."

"Gwen," he says finally, without further comment. My name sounds faint under the mask, like "when." I'm startled, exposed by his acuity.

First there was "what if." It was there as I ran a bath for my children, folded pyjamas hot from the dryer, as I rinsed potatoes in the sink and the silty water ran down the drain. I knew the sound of his truck's engine, could hear it from blocks away. I would wait for his headlights to sweep across my kitchen window as he turned at the corner. But then "what if" became "when," keeping me awake at night. "When," until Allen noticed the black circles under my eyes. The next word would have been "will," his name. Future simple, future catastrophic. I "will, will, will," like a three-year-old throwing a tantrum.

He has closed his eyes again, which is a relief. Without lashes, they are milky and bare, like pools just beginning to freeze over. I glance down at his hand, finding that this part of him, at least, is familiar. It is a precise hand, hairless, pale, curved slightly in anticipation of a task or pleasure. His nails are so clean they are bluish-white, more delicate than I expect from a man who worked with his hands for a living.

"Can I get you anything? Is there anything you want?" I ask. After a moment he raises his arm slightly off the bed and grins, or maybe it's the pain. He lifts the mask away from his face, drops it beside him.

"Everything I need is here," he whispers, directing my gaze to the IV running into his forearm.

"I'll read to you," I say and he nods.

I feel my voice thin and uncertain as I begin reading "The Lady of Shallott." I half expect him to tease me, as he always did at parties when I got too serious. "Gwen, sweetie, lighten up," he'd say, draping a strong arm around my shoulders. And I would suddenly feel the top of my head lift and I would stumble out of his reach, blaming the drinks.

When he pulled up beside me as I carried groceries home, his red truck was bright as a gash on the sleepy suburban street. Although he was smiling, there was an uncharacteristic remoteness about him, the blue eyes slightly unfocused. He was formal, more Wilhelm, his given name, than Will. I noticed the soil in the bed of his truck, packed back into the corners, seeded by the wind, green threads of life stretching up toward light.

"You are the one thing in this place that is spontaneous," I said. He looked puzzled. I pointed at the bed of his truck. "You're sprouting."

He turned around, the tendon of his neck long, tense, exposed. Then he laughed, turned back to me. "Get in," he said. A command, or the suggestion of someone who is used to getting his way.

My groceries were leaning cold against my bare legs, the uncooked chicken sending a chill up my spine. He told me about the inside of the houses we passed. Being a carpenter, he had been consulted at every neighbourhood party. Or perhaps he was told secrets by many of the wives. He knew who had a blood-red Jacuzzi, who put a skylight in their bedroom. He leaned toward me, hinting at darker secrets, too. He told me about two small holes above our neighbours' bed that went right through to the hallway. He said they might have been made with a fireplace poker.

"Does he hurt her?" I asked about a woman I barely knew. I would never be able to see her working in her garden without thinking about these two vicious little holes.

He didn't answer. His hands curved around the steering wheel, light, anticipatory. I told him about my first pregnancy, the apartment that was a narrow tunnel over a wallpaper store, with front door and back door opening out into a public hall.

"The light kept me up. Even though all I could see was the tiniest bit seeping in around the door frame. I kept thinking about the few feet between my living room and the street."

"And here you are, safe in suburbia."

"Safe, predictable and sound. Allen switched from Philosophy to Economics and the rest is history."

I had the distinct impression that I had somehow insulted him. I told him that Allen developed a sudden taste for the tangible: agriculture and airplanes, goods and services, a fair trade. The trade I made was to give up studying altogether. Four years of English Literature would have to do.

"So, does it do?" he asked me.

The next morning, after a night of high winds, I saw him again. I had been up at 3:00 a.m., wandering through the dark house. I leaned against the cold kitchen sink, watching twisters of garden debris, lit up by the porch light, come at the house, one after another, sending blown grit in through the screens. But it wasn't the wind that got me up, it was the energy in the wind, restless, humming, the walls too thin, sheer curtains bellying inward and flipping up.

He came just after I found the clematis vine torn from its support, a long purple spill lying on the front lawn. He showed me how to wrap its tiny tendrils around the trellis, how slender threads, strong as muscle, wrapped themselves around wood if you eased them into place.

"You just give them a nudge and they do what they want to do," he said. Then he positioned my bare feet in the soft garden soil, gathered the whole vine in his arms and draped the weight of it over my shoulders. His arms encircled me and I felt silence from head to toe, the solidity of his body shielding me from the far-off sounds of traffic, from the light wind through my summer clothes.

"Hold tight," he said as he wrapped tendrils and tied stems to the trellis with the string I had found in the garage. I couldn't tell if the cool, peppery smell was coming from him or from the purple blossoms tickling the back of my neck, drooping over the top of my head.

As he bent down, he made a mock gesture of supplication and laughed at the expression on my face.

"Guinivere," he said, more softly.

He started to tie the vine near my ankles, then level with my hips, moving up methodically, relieving me of the weight of the vine, working, knotting near my heart, my neck, and finally, tying clematis just behind my head, weaving some of my hair in with the leaves by accident, so that I was caught until he untangled me.

The delicacy of his fingers, his voice so soothing, coaxing, I couldn't help but let my own small wishes form.

My voice shakes as I read the lines:

Willows whiten, aspens quiver,
Little breezes dusk and shiver

But now, instead of laughing, as he would have when he was well, he expels his breath and waits. Gently, in words spun over one hundred years ago, the world floats slowly by. I rush past the funeral procession on its way to Camelot, but he opens his eyes at the lines, *'I am half sick of shadows,'* said *The Lady of Shallott,* and asks me to say it again.

He says, "Yeah," as though he's been waiting a long time to move on, even though it's been only a matter of months since he fell ill. And suddenly I'm crying through her weaving and her mirror, her loneliness and especially through the blooming water lily that brings the curse of love to her after she sees Sir Lancelot.

He says, "Thank you," when I'm finished, not formal, just weary. "That was nice." Sometime during the poem, he pressed the button on the morphine pump and now he begins to slip away from me, lying in a boat gliding down a river with the Lady, my voice trailing at a distance, carried easily across water.

The room wavers before my eyes, I drift up onto weak legs, my coat over my arm keeping me from floating high above his bed, and I hear my voice telling him that I love him. So simple, my voice more steady than I would have imagined.

He doesn't stir.

My heart is still pounding at the bus stop, still pounding as I lie next to Allen. At 2:00 a.m., his eyes suddenly open. I can see the corneas faintly blue by the light of the streetlight. Allen is a steady man, with round forthright eyes that seem to take in everything. They are either closed, in sleep, when he is usually turned away from me, or open. These are his two states of being. He's not given to bad dreams, or dreams of any kind, as far as I can tell. He says he doesn't remember them — the only evidence that they happen at all are the periodic erections I feel against me in the night. My hand has strayed to him in his sleep, has closed softly around the spongy warmth of his penis. It grows full as I move my hand and turn to press my breasts against his back. We do not speak, but I know Allen is fully awake when he enters me. I am open and quicker to come than I thought I would be. Afterward, I feel so agitated that I must get up and open the door to the hall. Doors have opened everywhere.

I replay scenes. A door opening to Will, standing there with a simmering intensity. He told me he had something to show me. My front hall had grown too charged, so I went, telling him that I would have to be back in two hours to pick up Amy from nursery school. Before I stepped up into the tall cab of his truck, I noticed the green sprouts growing in the corners of his truck bed had thickened to broad-leafed plants, every detail of the day vivid and searing. I'd never seen such green.

"What are you growing there? Lettuce?" I asked him. "Or marijuana? Something intoxicating or something nourishing?"

"I'm hoping for intoxication," he said.

We drove to a new development several kilometres away. The streets were named after pastoral fantasies: Sylvan Meadows Lane, Babbling Brook Way. Beyond the periphery were abandoned farm fields tangled with weeds, a barn with huge holes in its roof, as though it had been hit by meteorites or falling space debris. Soon it would be gone. Many of the houses looked finished, but the yards were still mud, messy uprooted Precambrian boulders, sewers raised a foot above the dirt track that would soon be a paved road. We drove further and came to a line of model homes with neatly landscaped yards.

"I've been building cupboards here. There's something you have to see."

"Body in the master bedroom?" I said, knowing even as I said it that "bedroom" was a dangerous word. But then, "body" was even more dangerous.

He took my arm, one of the only times he ever touched me. He steered me up the walkway of the vacant house. For a crazy moment, I thought maybe he was showing me the house where we would live. I heard an irresistible buzzing. I moved quickly in front of him and he caught up and held me back.

"Careful. No sudden movements." We stopped about fifteen feet from the small blue spruce in the front yard. I dropped to my knees to better see the swarm of honeybees, a twisting, boiling mass of wings, bodies, layer upon layer, forming a solid globe around the central branches. A few bees drifted around the bulging mass, the occasional one looping around our heads like a flying spark.

"They won't hurt us. They have bellies full of honey."

"Why are they here?"

"I've never seen this before, but I know what it is. It's a kind of bee reproduction, usually done in the spring. The old queen is somewhere in the centre, sending out sentries to find a new place. They're driven to do this. Incredible, isn't it? Any minute now, they'll sail off and start again. Too bad they won't make it."

"Why not?"

"Too late in the season. Any hive they build now won't be solid enough to keep them from freezing."

Freedom and chaos, I thought, a temporary swarming. That was all he was offering.

He took me inside the model home, opened the blond birch cabinets he had built. He slipped his hands along the beautiful sanded surface, showed me their empty depths.

On the way back, he said to me, "Tell me to stop." He would pull the truck over. I kept my face turned to the window, holding my breath so I wouldn't be able to smell him. It was August, the light was changing, growing filmier, afternoon light even in the morning.

"Tell me to stop," he said, more urgently.

When we reached the corner of our street, I said, "Stop," and got out of the truck.

I have to go back to the hospital. A repeat of last night. Jocelyn acknowledges me. Tonight, she looks slightly more rested.

"How are you today?" I ask, taking her hand again.

"My mother is here," she says simply.

"What about Will's mother?"

"Will's mother. What can I say? She'll be here for the funeral, when she can no longer remind him of how he failed her. Her brilliant son, the house-builder. I'll call her soon."

"Soon?"

"He's stronger today; he even ate some broth. First time

in five days. The doctor says that often happens after a brief reprieve."

She doesn't say *hope*, but I can see that even though the vigil might be longer, she sees this as a kind of gift.

"He won't see anyone that really matters to him now, except for me," she says, filling me with a bitter wave of jealousy.

"The children can't understand why he's turning them away. He says they give him a headache. I would have thought the morphine would take care of that."

"Maybe it's too painful, in another way," I say cautiously.

"You mean it's easier to push away than to let go? Yes, you're probably right about that. Damn him! He never really wants what he has." She's suddenly angry. "They're *his* children. They have the right to be loved, right to the end. I'm tired. I'm so tired."

Now she's crying. She's obviously at the end of her wits.

"I'll go now," I say, stepping away from her.

"No, you can read to him. Someone should be here and it can't always be me," she says and turns away.

"Gwen," he says softly when he sees me push tentatively through the curtain around his bed.

I'm embarrassed. I avert my eyes, glance down at my hands.

"Look ... at the flower you ... brought me. Full glory," he says. It takes a while because he has to pause for shallow breaths every couple of words. I can't bear to look at the bird of paradise; it is too flagrant. When I finally raise my eyes, I see the cords, the strange lumps of his neck, the harsh sheen of his skull.

"Are you going to read to me tonight?" he asks.

"If you want. What would you like to hear?"

"Everything. Just like last night," he tells me, directly. Some of his old self in that, a little of the tease, daring me to take it further, but there's sadness too.

"Is this ... right?" I ask, feeling the hair prickle on the back of my neck.

"Too late ... to worry about that," he says, rasping. His breath shortens, as if he has more to say, but after a long silence, he pushes the button on the morphine pump and sinks lower, or maybe only flatter, in the bed.

"You want me to say it again?" I laugh, I can't help it, and the tears blur along the rims of my eyes.

"I want you ... to," he says.

"Remember that time we ran into each other last Christmas?"

He closes his eyes. "Maybe," he says.

I can see that he doesn't remember. I tell him it was mild and his coat was undone at the top. I wanted to put my lips there, on his throat.

"Tell me more" he says.

"No," I say, with my hands folded in my lap. I look at him and suddenly he is unchanged, sleek and brimming with graceful masculinity. But then something overtakes him and he releases himself back into his own weariness. Once again there is the hairless sunken throat, the yellow skin. He closes his eyes and says, "I want you ... to tell me."

"Tell you what?"

"Tell me —"

"I can't."

"— what you imagined," he says, slurring his speech. Perhaps he pushed the button on the pump again. He seems to be drifting off.

I tell him I pictured us at Cedar Point, in the grass on the riverbank. The weight of him.

He's lying back. Perhaps he is already unconscious.

"What do you want?" I ask him. He looks at me, but his eyes have grown less intense. The drugs taking over.

"What do you want?" I ask again, knowing that I would do anything to bring him back.

"Nothing," he says almost under his breath. I look down at the book in my lap.

"Tennyson then." Suddenly all the poems seem to be about death, not love after all.

"'The Lotus-Eaters'," I say. He's moved beyond me again.

"Courage!" he said, and pointed toward the land,
"This mounting wave will roll us shoreward soon."

I journey into the shadowed glades drugged with flowers, wandering along streams, a place I've never been before.

Most weary seemed the sea, weary the oar,
Weary the wandering fields of barren foam.
Then someone said, "We will return no more;"

A slippery rasping sound and I look up. Will's eyes are open and unfocused. Then a smooth breath.

"There. That tree. An echo," he says. I lean closer, leaning on the metal rail between us.

"What? What did you say, Will?"

"A mistake," he says. "Not that wood. What's wrong with you?"

His voice is smoother and more fluent. He seems to have more air.

"No. Not a mistake," I say, the panic rising in my throat. He drowses for a minute and then grows restless again.

"Too bright," he says. "The echo. Listen to that." I hear a beating in my left ear. My breath is caught in an endless loop under my sternum.

"Watch out. Too shiny, too shiny. Cover your ears. Would you take a look at that. Beautiful," he says.

"I see the river. You're under the trees with me. I'll come with you," I say. A pause. He drowses for a moment, then presses the pump again. He seems to be waiting. After a minute, he's restless again.

"More," he says, almost a rasp.

"Yes. All right, yes," I say. I tell him that I knew what his hands would be like, light and precise on my breasts. It was always evening and the air was cool off the river. I would be torn between wanting it to happen quickly and wanting it to take all night.

"Your mouth ..." I say and stop.

"More," he says again, more urgent this time, twisting slightly and coming to rest against the silver bars of his bed.

I tell him about the depth and temperature of his mouth, the only way I can enter him. I tell him what it feels like when he is inside me and how I can't bear even a moment of withdrawal. I tell him I always want all of him back right away. I tell him that his thrusts have to be complete, but not hard.

I'm saying the word "swollen" when she interrupts.

"So, you've managed to put him to sleep," Jocelyn says. I must have been whispering softly because his wife only touches my shoulder. Half of me is still lost in the forest.

I jump, knocking the open book of poems off my lap with a bang that seems to echo down all the long corridors.

"I'll leave," I say immediately.

"That's good of you to read to him. I don't want him to be alone," she says as she sinks into my chair. "I don't want to be alone, either," she adds, her voice catching.

"It's late," I say, putting my arm into the wrong sleeve of my coat. "Do you usually come back this late?"

She looks up at me and her forehead crumples again. Tears fill her eyes.

"It could be tonight," she says, looking at Will. "I'm staying through the night. They told me it could be tonight."

"But he was better today," I protest.

"His system's shutting down. The body stops fighting itself. That's what they say," and she takes his hand. He responds, reaches out with his other hand until both are around her wrist. She gasps at the strength of his grip.

"More," he says again.

She leans to him and says softly, "What's that, Will? What do you want?"

"More," he says again.

"I heard you that time. Morphine. What's wrong with the morphine?" she says as she stands up to check the tubes connecting him to various instruments and machines around the bed.

"He's saying something about the morphine," she tells me. She runs her fingers along the thin tube running behind his back. She runs to call the nurse as he trembles, curled and closed as a shell.

How to sleep, startled in unguarded moments by something that feels like joy, then humiliation, then joy again. Keeping the door open, thinking I see a man standing there blocking the light from the hall. I do not sleep well, but dream anyway. That forest, far off through the trees, and a procession of mourners, all clothed in black. A sweltering summer day. I look down and find that I am naked. He's there alive and I want to get closer, but I'm not dressed for a funeral.

The phone doesn't ring. Surely she would call. I was the last one to see him conscious. I check with the hospital at noon. Still alive. His death is now only half of what I fear. I fear the phone not ringing. I fear the phone ringing and hearing her voice, icy and thin, saying, "How long has it been going on? Two years? Three? No point keeping secrets now."

Her voice and the dead space on the line after she hangs up.

I wait until Erica is in her room doing homework and Amy is settled before a video of *The Little Mermaid*, a treat I usually save for days she is sick. Allen pulls into the driveway as I step from the front step to the curving brick path we laid the year before last, muffled now with snow.

"Were you waiting for me?" he asks. "Are you on your way somewhere?"

I feel caught, focus on the place where his scarf rests against his throat. It's the dark wine-coloured scarf I gave him last Christmas. He's a solid man, dependable, wearing a grey overcoat, a grownup, and suddenly I'm fourteen, formulating a lie.

"I'm going back to the hospital," I decide to tell him, hoping my agitation doesn't show. "Joss asked me to."

He grimaces, shakes his head and I brace for his anger.

"I don't know how you do it."

"Do what?" I ask, waiting.

"Spend time there. I hate hospitals, the way they smell. How is he?"

"Out of it. Not really conscious, but it helps Jocelyn to know that when she has to leave in the evening for the kids, he's not by himself."

He steps forward and kisses me on the forehead. When he pulls back, the wet mark of his lips sings in the cold on my skin with a vivid, high note of almost-pain.

"You're a better neighbour than I am. I'll keep your dinner warm."

I'm still standing in the driveway when he reaches the door, his back to me, illuminated in a warm band of light that opens, then narrows again. I hear him inside, calling the children, one, then the other, and Amy's high squeal as he lifts her and swings her around. Now is the time to walk to the door, open it and step back inside. But I don't. I'm *stepping out*. I watch my feet, one step in front of the next, and am halfway down the street before I realize I could have taken the car, still warm from Allen's commute home. I don't need to be standing out on a dark street corner, freezing, waiting for an infrequent bus. But it swings around the corner, all long and lit, as if bidden from the deepest reaches of my unconscious.

Soon we pass out of the suburbs, onto the lighted, snowy streets, arc over the bridge, the river beneath black and thick, slowing down. Nothing in my hands, no flowers, no books.

A nurse knocks discreetly on his closed hospital door. When Jocelyn faces me finally, she seems calm.

"Gwen," she says, holding both my hands, "You've been a good friend. Thank you for making it easier for him and for me, too. Maybe someday I'll be able to return your kindness. But I hope not. I wouldn't wish on you a loss like this."

I wince at the irony of what she is saying. She places her cool hand on my forehead as though she senses the burning that rages there. Then she puts her arms around my neck, burying her face in my shoulder.

"He slipped into a coma early this morning. It won't be long now. Everyone else has gone home. I'm going to stay."

My face presses against her hair. I'm crying along with her, holding her softness against me, the body he has loved in my arms.

AUGURIES

The birds wake him after midnight. Standing at the bedroom window, he can't see them in the trees, but he knows they must be the flock of small black birds that congregate in the afternoons near the hospital. They shout harshly in the darkness; he is surprised lights aren't going on up and down his street. He often sees them in the afternoons when he's driving home from work. They line the spreading limbs of a diseased elm before soaring off like a huge black scarf blown by the wind. Everyone entering or leaving the hospital stops and looks upward uneasily, as though feeling the air disturbed by black wings on their faces. Normally the birds do not travel beyond their usual haunt, bordered by thorn and willow thickets to the north, taking in the broad parking lots of the hospital and the towering power lines.

Meaghan doesn't stir in her sleep. She lies on her back with one arm over her head, palm open, face turned sideways on the pillow. The cold moonlight coming through the half-opened blinds falls across her chest in sharp lines. Her aureoles are dark in this light. He wonders if they would feel cold to his lips, misted with blue shadows, like plums. The birds have not awakened her. Suddenly, they are silent. He slips back into bed beside her, adjusting the comforter above her bare shoulders, moving in close to bury his nose in her reddish hair and inhale her familiar scent, a meadow in June, simmering with life.

For the first time since the moment two weeks ago when he first felt the hard spot during lovemaking, he lightly moves his hand across her stomach and up, cupping her breast. She sighs once, a long exhalation. He presses softly near the warmth of her armpit. It is still there, a hard mass, rigid in the watery weight of her flesh. He pushes, it pushes back, more determined to make its presence known. He places his finger on it, expecting a pulse, but there is nothing but this hard immovable fact.

"Don't," she says, her voice definite, with no trace of sleepiness. Perhaps she has been lying beside him, listening to the birds. He pulls his hand back, suddenly ashamed. "I'm sorry. I'm so sorry," he says.

"No, it's OK. But I'll have enough of that today. From you I need something different."

She draws his hand down between her legs. He is startled by the silky complications beneath his fingers.

"Are you sure? This feels weird," he says, but even as he says it he feels the sheets grow smoother, cooler and more voluptuous against his genitals.

"You mean what's in store today? Or your shameless indulgence of my body's needs?" Although this is her characteristic way of speaking, she says this wistfully, her face now turned toward him in the dark. He senses her tension and touches her until he feels something release. Then, almost imperceptibly, her hips start to move and loosen. He never grows tired of the way she yields to forces he can't even perceive, water, currents of air.

He loves to walk beside her and watch the motion of her breasts. The complete guilelessness arouses him. She caught him, last Easter, as they walked down the street where her parents lived, needing a little respite from the hothouse atmosphere of holiday visiting. She glanced sideways at him, then further down.

"Get rid of it. I grew up on this street!" she told him. "You should be proud," he said. "To have your husband of fifteen years walk down the street like this." He pulled her close and felt her arms slide around him. She never blushed.

Now he says, "You couldn't sleep either? Did you hear the birds?"

"Birds. Oh, love, was it the lark or the nightingale?"

"Not crows, maybe starlings or grackles."

"Vultures. Maybe we've reached the vulture stage in our marriage," she says. Then there is silence between them when the meaning of this hits home.

A bird brought them together. Twenty years ago, when they were students, they had both worked at a French restaurant in the old part of the city where produce stalls and agricultural feed stores mingled with upscale urban restaurants and art galleries. The restaurant served crepes for breakfast, dinner and dessert. He was the only male waiter, hired by a female manager who wanted to make a point in the Seventies, the halcyon days of feminism. The manager had moved on, but he remained, the women swirling around him in their low-cut white blouses. They carried hot plates in their hands, brushing against him in the narrow confines of the kitchen, the scent of them and the smell of food, overripe remains drugging him into inefficiency. He was always hungry. Meaghan was one of these women, but he had not differentiated her from the lovely haze of others around him.

They were both scheduled to work Mother's Day, a notoriously unpleasant day. From table to table the mood shifted, one family high-spirited, another seething with resentment. That afternoon, a young woman and two men were in a far booth, obviously on the tail end of a long night out. She was beautiful, a flashing red mouth, dishevelled hair falling to her shoulders, slender pale knees barely touching under the table. He wondered which of the men had fucked her. He couldn't keep his eyes off her, went out of his way to switch sections so he could see her up close.

She ordered eggs and toast. There was petulance, an irritated static, when he told her they served only crepes. She left without so much as a glance at him.

He saw her again later that day, waiting to be seated, still wearing the same short, black cocktail dress. Meaghan made her way over to her. The crowd had started to thin out a little. She said something and Meaghan leaned toward her. Their hands seemed to meet and then Meaghan cried out. The other woman disappeared.

Then Meaghan laughed and he heard the lovely whip-poorwill cadence of it, her inner life revealed to him where five minutes earlier she had been a quiet young woman, taller than he usually liked women to be, a woman he noticed mostly to avoid colliding with in the kitchen.

She held a small yellow duckling out to him. It was shifting awkwardly on its webbed feet, its beak opening and closing with a soft high-pitched cry.

"She put it right into my hands," she said to him. "She told me to give her a call when I had some eggs."

One of the mothers at a table offered a gift box, soft with cotton. The duckling spent the rest of the shift in the staff washroom before he and Meaghan took it to his apartment. Instead of returning the duckling to the stall on the street where it had probably been bought, they decided they would take it to his brother's acreage in the hills outside the city.

"Promise me it won't end up on someone's plate," she said.

"Spoken like a true service professional. This little thing would hardly make a mouthful."

"But that will change. If I have anything to do with it." She smiled at him, her eyes fierce.

"Don't worry. My brother runs a charity farm. He's vegetarian."

"Are you sure you're related?"

"Why do you say that?"

"These elegant little crepes don't satisfy you. Twenty minutes after a break, you're on the prowl," she said.

He looked at her closely. She didn't shrink back from his gaze. For the remainder of the day they played with the duck, nuzzled it, scratched its tiny boned neck, fed it bread crusts soaked in milk. She said, "You live the life of a bachelor," while she looked through his fridge, her way of inquiring about his availability. He agreed, smiling at her. He eased a Styrofoam container from the back of the fridge and handed it to her.

"This is how much of a bachelor I really am."

She opened it and laughed, holding the container steady. "Lovely. Worms. Was this once edible?"

"It still is. I feed these to my oscars." She was puzzled. "Large tropical fish. I'll show you."

He led her to his bedroom. The bed was low to the floor and floating just above it was a restful lagoon of green light.

As night came on, they lay beneath the aquarium. They were afraid of crushing the duckling, so they put it in the bathroom. Its piping cries echoed against white tile, far off, like the voices of the children they would have one day. In the golden watery light, her throat glowed. His fish were larger than his hands, unhurried, and their shadows moved across her face. As more of her skin was revealed, the light intensified until it seemed that it originated from her body and not from the aquarium at all.

Later, when she rose to leave, she said, "You never have to worry about me preferring your roommate, Oscar."

And so it started, the way her words could flatter him and amuse him at the same time. The duckling had a long life. On the weekends they travelled up to the farm by bus, walking the seven miles from the highway in the dark. They stopped in the gravel quarry to kiss and sometimes make love. It was not the softest place, but it was the brightest, the limestone reflecting moonlight. He wanted to see her when he touched her; through the years, that had not changed. The quarry was scooped out of the dark, tangled hills, and no matter how unforgiving the surface, they found a way to mould their bodies to one another. He thought of this time as the most magical and benevolent of his life.

They arrived late at his brother's farm, the duckling in its box quieted by the cool still air. He took her hand and led her to the edge of the pond where he knew the ducks waited out the night. She didn't want to let go, but he convinced her that instinct would take over. He put his hands around hers holding the duckling and together they bent and released the soft warmth from their grasp. They knew the possibility of loss for the first time, an emptiness in their hands, cold and elusive. But they forgot loss when they were awakened at dawn by the fluted crowing of ornamental roosters in the trees around the house. Meaghan looked out the window, saw their long graceful tails, red and green, hanging from low limbs of cedar trees that had been allowed to grow wild.

"I think I'm dreaming. Or maybe I've died and gone to heaven. What is this place?" she said.

His brother, Bernard, collected unusual animals of all kinds, red-legged pheasants, exotic breeds of chickens, pampered and fluffed on their perches. From the window they could even see a spectacular rack of antlers moving down from the forest. He told Meaghan about Bernard's reputation for taking in wounded animals. The farm was in an area where marginal farmland within commuting distance of the city was bought by hobby farmers. The injured buck had been brought to him tranquillized in the back of a shiny new truck. Now it moved slowly on three legs toward the awakening sounds of the house. Bernard stood on the edge of the forest, reaching up his hand to scratch the buck's neck. He heard Meaghan's small laugh of delight.

His brother's oasis of birdcalls and undulating meadow intersected by gentle streams, seized from the rugged hills that towered above the farm, was where he and Meaghan established their tranquil, coherent life. He took her for long walks that first time, following the borders of fields and sloping banks of a slow, brown creek, soaking their pant legs in swampy spots. He watched her plant her sure feet just ahead of him, content to let her set the pace. And then she turned toward the forest, led him onto rougher terrain where the small green poplar leaves shook, scattering fragmentary light onto the forest floor. "Sorry," she kept saying, as small branches lashed him, but he didn't pull back, knew he wouldn't pull back. Whatever came at him, sudden and stinging, was worth the pleasure of being so near he could reach out and touch her.

They returned near dusk. Bernard stood on the front porch, watching them walk across the grassy field, leaving footprints in the dew. That evening, Bernard seemed smaller, as though he had pulled more deeply into himself when Meaghan was in the room.

"Don't let her go," Bernard said to him when Meaghan

had gone upstairs for a sweater. They were brothers again, wrestling and ricocheting off each other's energy. Bernard won this time, swinging his arm and fastening him in a choke hold from behind.

"Hold on tight," he said.

As the months passed, he and Meaghan lost the ability to distinguish the duck that had brought them together from all the others. Years later, a fox or fisher came down from the hills and swept all the ducks out of the pond. They vanished without a trace, but he and Meaghan were already married by then and it was years later that Meaghan thought to ask Bernard what ever became of the duckling they had brought up from the city.

Their son and daughter know nothing of the day ahead. They leave for school in the usual panic of finding matching socks, bitter and inconsequential disputes over who will take the dog to the park across the street. He catches the shadow of worry on Meaghan's face, but she looks up and smiles reassuringly, the two pale heads of their children between them. She is still wearing her bathrobe, thick blue terry cloth that holds the dampness after her shower.

When the children leave, she clears the table and he asks her why she isn't dressed.

"I haven't decided what to wear," she says.

"Does it matter? You won't be wearing your clothes when they do it."

"I don't want to wear anything I like because I may never want to wear it again. I can't wear anything I don't like because that's like tempting fate. Risking human sacrifice." She laughs.

She has laughed more in the last week than at any time since the early weeks of their relationship. Last evening, they heard a bell ringing in the street, an old-fashioned one swung hard and steady by a man pulling a cart. She sat with her head in her hands and laughed when he told her the man was a knife-sharpener, the first time either of them had seen one since childhood.

He stood with their children in the street, passing their knives to him, one by one, to be sharpened. Their daughter held out her hand to the sparks thrown off the grinding stone, thinking they were as benign as sparklers, and winced when she touched the heat of the newly sharpened blade. He took the knives away before they walked back to the house, holding them upright like a bouquet of flowers, far above the children's heads. Meaghan reached out her hands for them just inside the door.

"How lovely and so appropriate," she said.

Her bravery amazed him. Her strength, her sheer endurance, as when she gave birth, made him realize his own cowardice. The other new fathers in the hospital corridors had had the same shaken look and avoided meeting one another's eyes.

He picks up the garbage, carrying it to the front door and down the front steps. He hears a tapping on the living room window. She points with her index finger, first to his left, then his right. She is suggesting he pick up the litter on the lawn, a piece of plastic, old newspapers that have blown into the yard. Their neighbours had put out recycling boxes and now the driveway is strewn with detritus swept in by wind the night before.

He stoops to pick up sodden paper, retrieves stained flyers, and, strange for a morning in late September, crumpled Christmas wrapping paper, a little town wrapped in snow and starlight repeated over and over again. He wonders what their life will be like by Christmas. He wants a sleepy succession of years, each one similar to the last.

He has been standing with the wrapping paper in his hand when her tap on the glass startles him. He looks up to see her gazing at him, her grey eyes a little tired, her hair lightening to a brighter shade of copper as it lifts, drying from her shoulders. There have been moments all through their lives together when he could see her clearly, her very essence. When they were younger, this happened most often during sex. Her body was a translucent tunnel he travelled until he reached that breathless moment when he recognized her beneath the suddenly still water of her eyes. When the children were young, it happened less frequently, but now these moments arrive again, surprising in their suddenness, random and disconnected from sex. And here it is, a startling glimpse of her vulnerability. He knows that she feels it, too, an intensity heightened by the synchronicity between them.

She points again to something behind him. He grins, sinks to his knee, puts one hand over his heart, extending the other toward her in an exaggerated posture of courtship. She laughs and quickly unties her bathrobe, holding it open, bringing him quickly to his feet to look behind him to see who might be watching. She blows him a kiss and steps back out of the bright light, her white skin fading from view. The way she glides away from the glass reminds him of the oscars he had so long ago, their shadows passing across her on that night they first slept together. The image that follows disturbs him, but once fully formed, cannot be erased.

Perhaps he had been neglecting the tank, forgetting to change the water regularly. During the first month of their relationship, his oscars grew sick and the water seemed to thicken, took on a slightly slippery look. White lesions appeared on their sides, and something, not scales, something that resembled skin, hung from them like shredded wallpaper.

He dropped a ping-pong ball into the tank. The fish didn't respond, but hovered motionless near the bottom. Usually they were active, rearranging rocks, nuzzling the ball as it bobbed from side to side. They let the worms he dropped to the surface filter through the water like falling leaves before opening their mouths. They had no energy, no instinct to chase. He had them trained to eat out of his hands, but he didn't want to immerse his hands in the cloying water. Normally the two large fish let him rub them on the belly, just above the fin. Their bodies were slick and warm and vaguely bumpy, but he didn't want to touch them now. He tried a succession of drops, but day after day they remained immobile, obviously deteriorating.

He never told her what he did, but one day she squatted, face close to the empty aquarium left on the stairs outside his kitchen, and said, "You mean they died, just like that?"

"Once fish get sick, they go pretty fast."

"Did you try medicine? What did you do to them?" she asked, looking up at him, angry. He didn't answer her, knew in that moment that what she was insinuating was true. He hadn't tried hard enough. The elaborate process of setting up a sterile hospital tank was too much effort, distracted him from her.

"I'll get more. Fish don't live forever."

"It's the easiest thing in the world to throw something away," she said, catching his eye. "Everything is disposable, isn't it?" She looked away from him when he didn't respond.

"C'mon. We'll be late," he said after an uncomfortable silence and took her by the elbow, directed her down the stairs. She pulled herself away from him, not physically, but psychically, a chill of space between them.

They were on their way to work the same shift at the restaurant and he had been looking forward to the energy and anonymity of working alongside her, the electricity created by a thousand near collisions with other women in the kitchen, countless quick smiles and flirtations. They swirled together and apart, carried along on the bright current that he found so erotic, his anticipation growing more acute until they found themselves alone again.

When they came home, he saw the spot just beyond the parked cars where he had buried the fish. There were two perfectly symmetrical holes in the disturbed ground, raw and dark. His careful disguise of dried leaves was no match for the sharp noses of neighbourhood dogs.

"You are such a prude," she says. "You jumped up the second I flashed you. Do you really think anyone would be interested in my middle-aged body?"

"Who's complaining now," he says, untying her bathrobe again, kissing her collarbone, slipping his hands along her straight, long back. She leans heavily against him, the soft warmth of her breasts pressing a wave of sadness into his chest. He feels himself pulling back. She speaks into his neck.

"Not yet," she says, tightening her arms around him more firmly.

He holds her and they stand a long time at the living room window. Neither of them is going to work, so the morning has some of the timelessness but none of the pleasure he associates with holidays. They aren't setting out for some new adventure, with her long-fingered hand, its plain gold band, on his thigh for him and no one else to see.

Over the curving shape of her head, he stares at the black power lines they have lived beneath for seven years. She walks the dog under them every evening. Beyond the power lines and a thin fringe of trees is the hospital. For seven years, the hospital has had nothing to do with them.

A dull thumping sound, then a noise as intrusive as an airborne lawnmower moves over the roof of their house, blades cutting swaths in the air. The noise intensifies and she draws away from him.

"God, I hate that sound," she says, turning toward the window. They watch the yellow air ambulance hover above the hospital and slowly fall out of view. The rasping of the blades continues for several minutes.

"I used to sleep right through it, but now I think car wreck, plane crash, brain haemorrhages, pick your tragedy."

"I think of you in labour. You were baking a cake in the middle of the night."

She turns to him.

"Our bedroom was right beside the kitchen. It's hard to believe we lived in a place so small. The sound of the spoon hitting the side of the metal bowl woke me up. I was dreaming of flying in a war. The ground was on fire and then I awoke and knew it was time."

"You never told me that. Never," she says, walking to the kitchen to pour a glass of water. The water in her hand, clear as it is, might have brought them to this moment, the smoke from the hospital incinerator, the power lines, the microwave oven, the clock radio by their bed, the strong light that fades the umbrella in the backyard, the perfect green of their lawn, the smooth, unblemished passage of their lives.

She is turned away from him when she says, "I'm going to have it off if it's cancer. Can you live with that?" Her voice is abrupt, self-protective.

"Yes. You'd do the same for me."

She turns toward him then, smiling, and places her hands on his chest.

"It's not so bad having a lover without breasts. All these years, I haven't missed a thing. Not a thing," she repeats.

They stand like that for a time, gazing into each other's eyes, something she has taught him to do. He doesn't rush her, waits until she breaks the rhythm of her breathing and looks down, surprised to see that she isn't yet dressed.

"We could walk there. You might as well enjoy what you can of the morning," he offers. He can come back and get the car while she is in recovery.

"Maybe the air ambulance could drop a line," she says and laughs. "Now that would be a sight. I'd better wear pants."

They cross the street, ignoring the dog's nails scratching on the living room window. The black birds are gone from the wires, but they can hear small flutings of songbirds in the wood lot, the thickets of thorn bushes and new-growth trees held back by a chain-link fence. They follow a meandering earth. Footprints and serpentine trails left by bicycles run endlessly ahead of them. To their right, metal towers holding up the power lines rise far above the neighbourhood. Most are silent, but every so often they pass one that hums with a deep electric charge.

"Strange," she says, "to walk there with nothing but the clothes on your back. Sooner or later we're all brought to this. What's that proverb? Something like, 'We enter and leave life without pockets.'"

"I've never heard that before," he says. "What does it mean?"

"It means we only have this time, this morning, so we'd better enjoy it." Then she laughs, "Surely you can wine me and dine me a few more times, even without all my body parts."

Milkweed lines the crooked path. The autumn dew did not burn off easily and it is slick, marked with the small scurrying tracks of animals who were busy through the night. Ahead is the asphalt path that nurses use to travel from home to hospital and back again at all hours of the day and night. Yellow signs depicting a giant eye and a camera are posted on every light post warning of around-the-clock vigilance, but by day, the path seems harmless enough.

"There it is. I'm not quite ready for this. Let's stop a minute," she says.

"This is just a little detour," he tells her. "We'll be fine."

"We?"

They stop walking. Purple milkweed blossoms, encapsulated in fat curved crescents, are covered with goose bumps, like green skin. Soon the pods will toughen, crack and allow the chilled autumn air to scoop out their contents. He pulls a pod free and places it in her hand. She reaches up and touches his face before she slowly peels the tough skin and opens it like a pomegranate. Once she has unpleated the neatly folded seeds, she blows and sparkly white threads swirl free around them, soft and gentle on their faces as the wings of angels.

BLOODLINES

Gerard moves up close behind me as I'm at the sink, where the water is bubbling and shimmering over my hands, and he whispers, "I'll drop Zoe off at the preschool and be back for you. Turn off your modem, fax machine, everything."

He leans against me and the contrast between his solid body, suited for work, and mine, so flimsily covered by a dressing gown, leaves me coated in a film of heat.

"You're out of reach for the morning. Mechanical malfunction," he murmurs.

"And what about you?" I ask, turning and putting my arms around him. He's already been to work and back this morning. Julie rolls her eyes, picks up her book bag and heads out the door, slipping out of my grasp, as she always does when I reach to kiss the top of her head. Zoe sits transfixed before her cereal bowl, watching us.

"A fire in a factory in Japan, probably caused by that earthquake a few weeks ago. The price of RAM is going

87

through the roof, so I think we can afford a morning off."

"A windfall, huh? Never let an opportunity pass."

"Never," he says and lifts me off my feet. I cry out, then laugh. Zoe looks alarmed.

Sometimes when we have a rare morning alone, we are raucous. But, today, back in bed, we are shaken by how the mood suddenly changes to tenderness. The light catches the fine, curled hairs of his chest. Before I shift, he knows he's grown too heavy and slowly pulls away. This is my least favourite moment, this sudden emptiness so forlorn, but the sweet spring air tickles the bottoms of our feet as we lie facing the window. He bends down and kisses me on the mouth and the moody moment passes.

We dress, lock the door behind us, walk hand in hand in the direction of the preschool. We pass an elderly couple pulling their ailing golden retriever in a wagon. The man lifts the dog from its quilted nest of pink and yellow. He bends over, holding the dog's hips in his hands, half lifting her as she staggers to the lush grass of our neighbour's front yard. His wife watches intently with a washcloth in one hand, a plastic bag in the other.

Gerard says, "If I *ever* act like that, go ahead, arrange a quick euthanasia."

"No way. You're in this for the long haul," I say. "Or the long push."

The gardens along our quiet street are ringing with colour, each one unique, a carefully designed arrangement of spring blooms and flowering trees. Pale blue tulips, lilac shrubs in unusual hues, nothing as ordinary as rangy, pale lilacs set in unimaginative straight lines. Yet they don't seem to have the wild, airborne sweetness of the ones of my youth.

We see the steeple of the church rising needlelike above the vivid blur of green leaves. Except for the occasional funeral, the sanctuary itself sits empty all week, but the basement is a hothouse of children's voices. Cries echo in the stairwell, then the preschool opens before us, a festival of red and white: Canadian flags and posters, balloons and streamers, children running on a sugar high, half-eaten red and white cupcakes littering every surface.

"What's this?" I yell to Irene, the director.

"Canada Day. A little early, but what the heck. They love it!" she yells back. "Oh, and sign that card for Terry, will you? She's leaving," she says, smiling at me.

I stand near shelves of toys and board books, holding a large homemade card. Someone has fastened red and white helium balloons to it with long ribbons. In order to sign it, I have to undo a slipknot that anchors the card to the leg of a chair. Tendrils of red and white ribbon have been curled with scissors and ripple down in lovely cascades, level with my knees. I vaguely register a small blond baby, barely walking, who leans on my leg and reaches out to tug on them.

The baby loses his balance and topples face first into the shelves. He lies on the floor, a sudden cry as blood seeps, then pours from the split skin on his forehead. I let go of the card in my hands and it pulls upward on the helium balloons and bumps against the ceiling. I rush to soothe him and his cries heave in my ear. His ribcage convulses; he feels as delicate as a baby bird, the tiny bones distinct beneath his jumper. I whisper, "Shhh, shhh," holding him. The warmth of his blood spreads on my arms, my chest. The morning's physical pleasure is still with me and I place my lips against his temple to comfort him. His blood tastes warm and sticky, like rust. The swirling mix of children and mothers part before me as I carry him toward a woman wearing sandals and khaki pants. She's one of the mothers I've never even talked to. She sweeps back her wavy hair, which is the warm colour of milky tea, a little too young for her narrow, critical face. Suddenly I remember her campaign against Disney videos. She wanted nature films instead.

"Is he yours?" I say once I'm within earshot. The wispy baby in my arms is whimpering now. She turns to me and gasps, which surprises me. She's the type who has seen it all, slept in chicken coops in South America, dug wells by hand in dusty villages. Irene runs for a pair of surgical gloves, but the mother quickly puts down the child she's carrying, expertly fishes gloves out of her purse and pulls them on with a violent snap. She snatches the baby out of my arms.

"Wash over there," Irene says to me. "*Now!*"

I watch the water run pink, then eventually clear. I wash the sleeves of my shirt, but the stain on my chest will have to wait. I turn back to see Gerard holding Zoe, talking in close, urgent tones to Irene. The mother sits with a can of frozen orange juice, wrapped in a cloth, held to the forehead of her baby. Everything has quieted down.

"This shirt has seen better days," I say. Zoe reaches out her arms for me.

"I'm kind of wet, honey," I tell her. I bend to kiss her on the forehead when Gerard suddenly turns away from me, moving Zoe out of reach.

"Mommy, I didn't finish my cupcake." Zoe looks confused, a little angry.

"Where did you leave it? I'll fetch it for you," I say, but Gerard says, "Don't. You shouldn't touch anything she puts in her mouth."

"He doesn't attend this school," Irene tells Gerard. "He's just visiting with his mom today. I can't control everything," she says irritably. I've never heard her voice as anything other than sweetness and light.

The mother looks up at me and says, "I'm sorry, but you'll need a shot. Gamma globulin."

I think she's said "goblins" and I laugh. She doesn't react and this chastens me, though she doesn't look particularly sorry. Her face has returned to its usual composure: concern just this side of disdain.

"Would you like me to pay for dry cleaning?" she asks. "You probably shouldn't wash it yourself."

The baby has calmed and dropped into a deep, exhausted sleep.

"You *will* need a shot," she says again.

"Why?"

"He's a carrier of hepatitis. It doesn't hurt. Just a shot in your hip."

Gerard doesn't say anything as we walk into the bright light of the street. The red stain on my chest is magnificent and we have two blocks to walk home. Even Zoe is quiet.

"That's a dramatic ending to a perfect morning," I say. Gerard doesn't answer. "People passing us will think you're a wife-beater." He still says nothing. "How would a child that young pick up hepatitis?" I say.

"He's from a Romanian orphanage," he finally responds.

"I wondered how she could have two children so close in age." I reach out and slip my arm through his, but he feels stiff, doesn't lean toward me.

"You should ask the doctor about something else," he says. "The baby has AIDS, too."

I'm travelling in the wrong direction, away from my home, through unfamiliar neighbourhoods, each seedier than the last, toward the hospital with the old vaulted ceilings and the psychiatric ward, the one with the infectious diseases department. This was Gerard's idea. He went into action, looking things up in the phone book, calling around before telling me, "You'll need the best possible early assessment. Ask for Dr. Aziz. I'll drive you there," but I told him I couldn't see the point of Zoe spending hours in the emergency waiting room.

As I pulled out of the driveway, I saw him standing at the living room window holding Zoe, framed by the gold silk valance and sheers. He and Zoe grew smaller and more shadowy, until I couldn't see them at all.

I could pretend I'm headed in the opposite direction, toward the hospital with the pastel birthing room and friendly nurses. But even there, engaged in the most mysterious and intimate act of my life, I was more alone than I'd ever been before. I was one, then the pain was so intense, I was nothing. Then love flooded me like an anaesthetic and we were two. I heard Gerard's voice, the voices of the nurses and doctor, hollow and insubstantial, as though they were travelling across water to reach me. Most of the time our bodies are too dull to perceive much of anything, but *this, this* was real. I've never described this to Gerard. How important it was to both of us then to be in control. I went far away from him when he was holding my wrists, gazing in my eyes, saying, "OK, slow your breathing. I'll count with you. One, two ... slow it down, good." The rent healed and I forgot.

A woman knocks on my car window at a red light in the part of town where once grand Victorian houses are now reduced to shabbiness. Her balding fur coat looks mangy and dried out in the late May sun, and at first I don't realize she's one of the homeless people who go car to car, collecting money. Gerard and I usually stare ahead, trying to avoid eye contact. She looms beside me, stooping to see inside. I'm flustered, my heart is pounding and I lower the automatic window to throw out my parking change. She bends over to pick up the change, slowly raises herself upright and thanks me in a very proper British accent.

"Thank you very much, ma'am. You're too kind," I hear just before the automatic window slides closed. Is she being sarcastic? An unpleasant wave of shame travels up the back of my neck and I grab a twenty-dollar bill from my purse. I put the car in park and step out into the street, hit by heat and exhaust, but she's two lanes over by now. Horns start to sound and cars pull out to get around me, a gleaming mass of impatient metal. She glances back to see the source of the commotion, meets my eye over the roofs of the cars and hurries away without looking back again.

The nurse at the desk looks at me suspiciously when I tell her I need to see a doctor.

"What can I do for you?" she asks. Obviously, I don't seem desperate, damaged or poor enough to warrant her time. Her attention is continuously pulled away by activity in the crowded room.

"I've been exposed to hepatitis and AIDS. A child bled on me."

"It's HIV," she says impatiently. "Bled on? Where's the child?" she asks, looking behind me crossly.

"Another hospital. He fell. He needed a few stitches."

"Was he *your* child? Where is he now?" And then I understand that she is worried about the child, not about me, who stands before her with matching suede purse and shoes.

"I've never seen him before. It was at a nursery school. He fell. I picked him up. I was told he was adopted from a Romanian orphanage."

"Which nursery school?" she persists. She doesn't give me so much as a second glance until she writes it down. "OK. Any eczema, open wounds? Any blood on your mucous membranes?" she asks.

"I tasted rust. Maybe some of his blood went in my mouth."

"In your mouth?" she looks up at me, incredulous. "You'll need a shot. Sorry, but you'll have to wait a while," and she turns away, dismissing me.

"I should see Dr. Aziz. He's the infectious diseases specialist," I tell her.

"I know who he is," she says. "You get the doctor on call. That's the way it works here."

A young man shrieks at the top of his lungs. "Stop it! It's moving up my arms!" I back away from her desk quickly, out of his reach. He's lunging from side to side. The nurse emerges from behind her counter, speaks firmly into his right ear.

"Can you hear me? Denny, can you hear what I'm saying?" She circles his flailing wrists with both her hands. He's stronger than she is and one hand flies up, hitting her in the mouth, but she doesn't flinch.

"We're going to stop it. Can you feel my hands? If you can feel my hands, then you're OK. Watch me. Look at me," she says and he calms slightly.

"I won't let go, I promise," she says, speaking rhythmically and walking backward, holding him by the hands, leading him away.

The afternoon passes like this: outraged cries of babies, coughs, resigned groans and the quick hissing sounds of prayer under the breath. No laughter. Every other sound a human being can make, except for laughter. A green undercurrent of nausea keeps me looking at my hands, the elasticity and rosiness of the skin. When it passes, I pick up a newspaper that has been left on the table. Whenever I lift my eyes, the people around me seem to have changed, but their misery remains the same.

I flip through the front section. I'm not up to the intricacies of an article on the human genome project, turn back to international news. There's a short article, two inches by two inches, about a little girl who drowned just off the shore in Holland. People on the beach tried to reach her by making a human chain, hand to hand, stretching out into the sea, but they couldn't make it long enough because some wouldn't join. The girl was dark-skinned, a refugee. "We've got too many. It's not our problem," someone said, interviewed at the scene afterwards. The photo beside the small story is grainy, taken from a helicopter or a high cliff. Dark figures in a line joined at the hands, then suddenly a flat horizon of endless water. The girl is already under water, out of reach.

A faint headache is insinuating itself behind my eyes. I try to focus on something in the distance, the clock, which now says 4:17, the scrap of old Christmas tinsel that glitters near the vent above our heads. Julie will be home from school by now. Time will pass and this will be an amusing story I'll tell at Gerard's Christmas party, leaving out the private parts, the sexual details that explain nothing, and everything, about how I ended up here.

The woman sitting across from me has a blue plastic clip on her nose. Blood is splattered down the front of her white shirt and she holds a bloodstained towel on her thick lap. Her eye is swollen shut, red and angry. Intermittently, tremors pass through her.

"Don't worry, the kids are great," a man says as he places a cup of coffee before her. I hear the petulance in his voice before it is replaced with solicitude. "It's a day off school, just like a holiday."

His knee jiggles fast and he's about to reach out for her hand, which is lying palm up in her lap, when the nurse blocks his way. She leans over and speaks to the woman, then leads her away, signalling him to take a seat. The only chair free is beside me. I recoil, but he continues to stand with the cup of coffee in his hand.

"You let her be," a voice beside me says. The man ignores it.

"You heard me. You let her be now."

I look beside me and see a middle-aged black woman with threads of grey running through her hair. Her face is angled up as though she is taking in the warmth of the sun. She has one of those faces that always seems to be smiling.

The man is tense as a spring and steps toward her, so close to me I can smell the simmering heat of his armpits. He points his finger in her face.

"What did you say?"

"Honour and cherish," she says.

He wants to strike out, his fuse is lit, and he raises the Styrofoam cup and holds it near his shoulder, ready to throw. She stares at him, saying, "In sickness and in health." His leg, just a few feet away from mine, is trembling. The cup explodes in his hand, spraying my legs and the woman's legs with hot, milky coffee. He throws the crushed cup in the woman's lap and storms away. She brushes it to the floor, turns to me and apologizes for the spots on my linen pants, but I can see she's taken most of it on her own legs. I'm still shaken when she hands me a tissue from her purse.

"When she's bled enough, she'll let him go," she says.

I close my eyes and try to even my breathing. The seat between the woman and me is empty, one of the few in the whole crowded room. Two dark children with rattling coughs climb over the backs of our chairs, shaking the whole row, occasionally bumping my arms.

"Get down, Cass, get down now. You're bothering that lady," the woman says to one of the children breathing heavily down my neck. But before they have done what she has told them to, she turns away to another, much younger child asleep on the other chair beside her. She lifts her onto her lap and the child glances up at me with frightened, bleary eyes. Zoe's age, yet she looks like a wizened old woman. Her skin is purplish brown, as though blanched with cold. Her hair is thin, sticking in tufts to her bony skull. It is obvious she has a fever. She looks away, slides down into the chair beside me and lays her head against the hard armrest close to my hand. I should find another seat in this crowded waiting room. I should not put my arm on the rest that supports her head, now filmed with her breath. Would I have bent to pick up this child? I suddenly ache, imagining Zoe, sick and frightened, lying impassively on this hard and ugly plastic chair, nobody reaching for her.

"This little piggy went to market," the woman says, reaching out and holding onto one tiny brown toe. Although it's a dry, sunny day outside, the child has been wearing blue rubber boots without socks. The boots lie tipped over on the floor, tiny Bugs Bunny icons near the rim. I remember Zoe's favourite Roadrunner shoes, how we found her wearing them in bed in the middle of the night. But it's hard to imagine this little girl with enough energy for favourites.

"And this little piggy stayed home," the woman continues. "This little piggy had roast beef. And this little piggy had none." She's eased a shy smile from the sick child, whose gums look swollen, mottled with pale spots.

"That's my beautiful girl," she tells her and strokes her head.

The two older children are starting to whine, asking for money for the vending machine. The woman beside me shushes them in such a no-nonsense way. I know better than to open my change purse and give them money. She takes scissors out of her plastic handbag and reaches for the newspaper I have left on the table, stained here and there with coffee. She tears off the front sheet and folds it over and over until it is a square. She cuts small slits and triangles along the edges of the paper, makes one, then another. The children unfold their snowflakes, so different and intricate, that I know this is a well-practised skill. I did this with Zoe on Valentine's Day. We cut doilies into lacy patterns, glued them to a velvety red heart. She cried as though her own heart was breaking when it ripped as she was writing her name, so we started again, but the pleasure was gone for her.

"They're crazy about snow," she tells me, noticing that I've been watching them unfold their snowflakes.

"Every day when they wake up, they want to know if it's going to snow. It's May, I tell them, but it makes no difference. Snow every day and they'd be happy."

"Where are you from?" I ask.

"From Haiti, ten years ago, but they came in January, after my daughter died." I shudder inwardly with the evenness of her tone. Words I can never imagine saying.

I hold the little one, the sick one, on my lap. For all the lightness of her bones, she leans heavily against me. She's hot in an unfamiliar way animals can be, with a different metabolism and life span. Her grandmother has gone to find the bathroom to blot the wet coffee from her skirt. This is the third time today I've felt another life, another body, so intimately connected to me, and this hot, damp weight is much more real than any other. Gerard and the morning that brought me here are from another life.

The nurse bends close to me, touches the child's forehead and tells me it's my turn. She smiles at me now. I'm starting to belong. Soon I'm led into a room, stepping around curtains the colour of pale skin. My partition contains only a high bed half covered by a rumpled sheet. I sit and wait again. The curtain continues to swing slightly as though it is breathing in and out, in and out. Only two or three feet away, another woman whimpers and shifts her body. She waits, too. Through the curtain, I will hear the awkward silence as she unbuttons her blouse for the stethoscope, or removes her clothes for whatever might be required.

When the curtain finally opens, it is as though I recognize him. The white of his coat gives his brown skin a dusky cast, as though he has been out in a windstorm in a sandy, barren place. His hair is lustrous black under the bright lights. His expression is kind, his movements certain and unhurried. After all the waiting, I'm glad he's finally here and I feel a small clenching in my chest. I hold my hand, the one with the wedding ring, out to him. He considers it a moment, reaches out and takes it in his own.

PITILESS

We walk with our daughter to the park after dusk. It's that time between winter and spring that no one has ever named. Nothing is shooting up new and vibrant yet, but every living thing that carries the memory of winter is starting to stir. Change is going to seize hold with a vengeance soon enough, but for now everything is held in a pause, timeless. We would prefer to walk on the riverbank instead of the paved path where bicycles veer like dark asteroids, missing us by inches, but the bank is still mushy, emitting terrible smells of sweet, bitter rot.

Just ahead, two men are lying on dead grass flattened by the weight of recent snow. I see their cigarettes, fireflies blinking, and as we walk closer I can make out the lines of their fishing rods straight out over the river. A dead carp, one no one would choose to eat, lies beside them. We have two golden ones at home in a bowl. Becky feeds them flaked food every day, talks to them when they kiss her fingers through the glass. The men on the shore lean back on their elbows. They have been here every night since it warmed up. We all have.

A young couple sits on the third park bench arguing. Last night they became silent when we walked by. Tonight they pay no attention to us.

I hear her say, "You dump your change on the table, then expect me to keep things clean." Her voice wheedles, irritated, as we move out of range.

"What are the odds?" my husband asks.

"Of what?"

"Of their marriage lasting?"

"Forever, if she learns a thing or two. I just steal your change, spend it on all my secret vices. You're none the wiser."

"Just poorer. What happened to the 'the richer' part you promised me?"

When we talk like this, Becky ignores us. Tonight, she's walking a few feet ahead along the river path, making me nervous about passing bikes. She's starting to move beyond our reach, then she retreats to be held safely in our arms.

Suddenly she's between us again, clinging to her father's leg, burying her face. He asks her what's wrong and she just points to the river. He squats down and asks her again.

"I saw a whale. It was big." She points out across the dark water. "I saw it come up for air."

He laughs and says, "The river is two feet deep. There are rabbits, but no whales. They live in the ocean far from here."

At the mention of rabbits, Becky perks up and asks if we can go see them. Ever since she saw the rapids just ahead, where the river is especially shallow, and called them rabbits, we have seen water in a new way, white and fluffy, leaping over rounded stones.

"It's too far in the dark," I tell her, "but we can go to the bridge."

Becky is three years old and likes best of all to be under the bridge where water drips down concrete walls, where the flapping of wings and pigeons' coos echo and the heavy traffic overhead thuds like a heartbeat.

Tonight, as she does every night, she sings at the top of her lungs, "If you're happy and you know it, clap your hands." Clap clap. Her high voice reverberates and echoes. Everyone in the park must hear her, but no one has let on, not the young couple, not the men fishing.

"If you're happy and you know it and you really want to show it, if you're happy and you know it, clap your hands," and we laugh and clap along.

I wonder if the man in the kilt hears the voice under the bridge. He is the other regular in the park. I quietly keep track of him when we're on our evening walks. I don't like him to get too close, but he stays near the shrubs and tall trees. He often lies flat on his back, then leaps up and climbs the large maple with silvery bark and one huge outstretched limb about eight feet off the ground. Sometimes he sits for an hour without moving. People walk beneath without noticing him, but I steer my husband and daughter away.

Becky looks around when we resurface from under the bridge and enter the dark park again.

"Where do you think the man in the skirt is?" she asks. I look around, then catch sight of him standing quietly some distance away under the maple, the moonlight illuminating the long underwear he always wears under his kilt.

She sees him, too, and asks, "Why does he wear that skirt? Is he a really a girl?"

This offers up the possibility of distraction, so I launch into descriptions of Scotland, foggy mountains and the wail of bagpipes.

"Now we know what Canadians wear under their kilts," my husband says and we laugh, but, of course, Becky doesn't get the joke. She's focused on the man, hears before we do the sound of his tense muttering. He's gesticulating, as though swarmed by biting insects. His voice is hissing, then growling. I can't make out very many words because he's spitting them out fast, voice hoarse. I hear "hurt." "Damn you." Then something about poisoning.

"Who is he talking to?" Becky asks. "Is he mad at some-body?"

"He's mad all right," my husband answers.

"Is he mad at me?" Becky asks, perturbed.

"No, sweetie. He has an illness that makes him act like that."

"Does he have a mom who takes care of him?"

I don't want her to know how pitiless the world can be, so I tell her that, yes, he has a mother. That seems to answer something for her and we walk on, moving out of range. She's singing to herself the winter song we should have left behind by now. "The more it snows, tiddly pom, the more

it goes, tiddly pom, the more it goes tiddly pom, on snow-
ing. How cold my toes ..." and the rest we know by heart.

"I wish they'd clear the parks out at night," I say to my
husband.

"That's a compassionate view, if I ever heard one," he says.

"You know what I mean. He could be dangerous."

"Only to himself. Relax, he's harmless."

But before these words are out of his mouth, we hear
the man in the skirt behind us, moving quickly in our direction. He starts to yell and we make out enough to know
he's yelling at us.

"You! You and your damn little girl!" The rest is almost
incoherent. He's furious, yelling and jabbing a finger in our
direction, fast and menacing, on feet that are surprisingly
deft. It's one long stream of vitriol. "Come out from behind
that thing on your face, fucking bastard, you and your
moustache, I can see you, I can see, don't hide, fucking little
tramp, I see what you've done, your little bitch, you think
I'll let you, no way, no way, I'll do you, you just try, you'll
see, I know, I know, that little bitch is full of it, what are you
looking at, goddamn you, what are you looking at, I'll teach
you not to stare ..." Becky is clinging to my leg. I have to
stop walking, which is the wrong thing to do.

"Pick her up," I tell my husband. "Let's go. Don't look at
him."

Then Becky starts to wail. The man in the skirt is close
enough for me to smell the rank odour of unwashed flesh.
He's leering at her, pointing and screeching now, "I'll tear
her lying little tongue out of her head, I know, I know what

you've done, you and your moustache …" All I hear then is Becky's hysterical crying. My husband strides toward him before he gets any closer. I can see he's on the verge of losing his temper. "You're scaring my daughter. Stop yelling right now. You're frightening her."

I call after him, panicking, "Be careful. Come back. Let's get out of here."

The man in the skirt is within striking distance of my husband when he suddenly stops ranting, turns around and walks away, still muttering to the tops of the dark trees.

Although we would rather go home now, we don't. We finish our nightly ritual with the hope that this will help Becky forget the encounter.

"We could go to Timportance," I say as though this has never occurred to me before. Becky's way of saying Tim Hortons. My heart is still beating, a hard beat, followed by several quick weaker beats, out of rhythm. I need coffee, something warm in my shaking hands.

"Timportance! Timportance!" she calls out, suddenly free of her tears, her jagged little sobs. She swings with each of our steps, far out like a pendulum between our two hands, sailing off into space, then bouncing back.

I dream about him. About the tree he sits in, a limb splitting off and crashing through our roof. I'm on my feet even before Becky calls out. I was surprised by how quickly she fell asleep tonight. And here is finally what I was expecting at bedtime. She's sitting up in bed when I open her door.

"The bad man is going to hurt me," she cries.

I climb in beside her, smooth her hair, whisper in her ear. "You're safe in bed. I'm here."

"Why does the bad man want to hurt me?" She's crying again, her forehead hot with nightmares she doesn't remember.

"He's not a bad man, just sick. He's gone now." But I'm angry at him, at psychiatric hospitals, at a city that lets men like him run wild in public places, climbing trees, eavesdropping on snatches of our lives, scaring children half to death.

"You should be sleeping. Your dad's asleep. Your fish are asleep in their bowl." I keep my voice low, hypnotic, trying to put her into a trance. But she sits bolt upright again.

"Where do my fish sleep? Do they lie on the bottom of the bowl or on the top?"

Amused despite how tired I am, I take note. Here is the explanation I can use when the end inevitably comes. They're not dead; they're just sleeping. They are having wonderful dreams of swimming in a long, wide river.

"Shhh. Just think of all the birds sleeping in the trees. Your grandmother is asleep. So is Kristin. The dog is asleep in Mr. McIntyre's house. The whole neighbourhood is dark and quiet. Everyone is sleeping."

She starts to drift off, then sits up.

"Is the man in the skirt asleep? Is he still up in that tree?" she asks. I take a different approach. Her favourite subject.

"What are you going to be when you grow up?" I ask.

"I'll be happy," she tells me, as she often does. "I'll believe people unless they lie over and over."

"Would you like to be a teacher like Eleanor? A doctor? A mommy, too?"

She thinks a moment. "I don't know," she says. "I won't be a kidnapper. Only people with bad parents are kidnappers. I'll never scare children."

I laugh and she puts her arms around me, tells me she loves me and suddenly drops into deep, untroubled sleep.

Tonight all of us are in our usual places. We are walking along the paved path, the couple are sitting on their park bench and the men are resting on their elbows, their fishing lines angled into the dark river. The frogs are singing very loudly in the shallow, soggy parts along the shore, springs starting to wind up. It's harder to catch the couple's conversation, but it's clear that the woman is still bitching and the young man, like last night, leans toward her sympathetically.

"It's scruffy," the young woman is saying as we pass by. "I think you should shave it off."

"Love is blind," my husband says. "And deaf. The poor idiot."

I turn and kiss him quickly on the mouth.

"That again," Becky says, exasperated, slapping me. As I take my mouth away, the spring air is soft and cool on my wet lips.

"I read somewhere that the chemicals in the brain that make you think you're in love last only three years. After that, you see what you've really got. Imagine the shock he has ahead."

"Don't tell me that. Becky is three now."

I saw the man in the kilt a few minutes ago. He was throwing the end of a fluorescent yellow rope up into the air and it kept falling beneath the large tree he always occupies. A lasso of some sort. Out of the corner of my eye, I see over and over the slash of faint yellow zigzagging through my field of vision, like the beginnings of a migraine. It makes me shudder a little. Sometimes just seeing something like that, some visual disturbance, will spur a headache. The moving lines of light I see before a headache are there whether my eyes are closed or open. But I can eliminate this jagged, disturbing light by turning my head the other way.

I touch my husband's arm and point to the river: "Oh, look. There's a muskrat." It glides so sensuously, so silently, that I want to follow, but when it climbs onto a rock it looks like a sewer rat. I say, "Let's follow this path to the road for a change. That's enough of a beautiful spring night for me."

Because we're changing the routine we follow every night, he asks, "Why? Aren't you feeling well?"

"I'm fine. I just don't like walking under the trees when it's this dark," I say, keeping any unpleasantness out of my voice.

I start to play the "I love you" game with Becky. "I love you more than all the frogs in the river," I tell her.

She laughs and says, "I can hear a lot of frogs."

"And that's how much I love you."

"I love you more than all the boots in the world," she says, happy to be wearing her new purple boots for the first time, even though it has not rained.

"I love you more than all the locusts in the Bible."

"Hey," my husband says, "that's way over her head."

"You're just jealous. Has any woman ever said she loves you more than pestilence?"

"I should hope you do. I take that sickness and health thing seriously."

"What's a locust?" Becky asks.

"A giant grasshopper," I say and jump once toward her, then tickle her ribs. She squeals and jumps ahead of us, then runs fast in the direction we usually take.

"Becky," I call. "Becky, we're going *this* way tonight. Come back right now!"

But she runs ahead, yelling, "Timportance! Timportance!"

Before I'm able to catch her, we hear her voice loud and high, a cry between fear and elation. I grab her hard around the arm and pull her away.

"Mommy, the man in the skirt is flying!" she cries.

My husband runs to us, yelling, "Jesus," wraps his arms around the man's white legs swaying off the ground beneath the tree.

"Oh, no! Oh, no!" he cries. I stand a distance away, my hand over our daughter's eyes.

"Go get help," he yells, gasping with the weight in his arms. My husband's face is pressed against the man's groin. "For Christ's sake, hurry up! I can't hold him up forever!" he yells, this time directly at me.

But if I move, Becky will see, so I stand quietly under the shadow of the tree. Becky stands transfixed beside me, even though I can feel her trembling against my leg. Her eyelashes sweep my palm as she blinks and I feel the heat from her open eyes in my cupped palms, as if she can see through my flesh.

The fishermen rush past me in the dark. One man works with my husband to lift the figure higher off the ground, almost up onto their shoulders, their legs buckling under the weight. My husband forgets me for a moment. He says, gasping with the exertion, "You'll have to climb the tree to cut him down. Hurry! My arms are getting tired."

Surprisingly, the heavier man is climbing the tree. I see him shimmy out along the limb where the rope is fastened, the bright flicker of his filleting knife held between his teeth. And then there is motion, the hanged man's white legs rise, then fall to earth. The couple from the park bench are here now, too, and rush forward into the darkness under the tree. The young woman gives terse commands, all the irritation gone from her voice.

"Turn him over. Hold his head back," she says, and then a sound like the cartoon sound we make when we blow air from our mouths onto our daughter's chubby stomach.

"It's no good. It's too late. I think his trachea is crushed," the young woman says. "It's too late," she says again, puts her head to the man's chest. "Maybe there's something still there. I'll try again," she says, more to herself than to us.

The man in the kilt is stretched out, inanimate, as though he has always been solid and unmoving, an object without will of its own. My husband lies, gasping, on the grass beside the woman, who is hunched over so close to him, it could be his body she's working on with her hands and mouth. It's an intimate position, almost obscene. He can't catch his breath. I don't want to listen. Perhaps he senses this because he suddenly focuses on me. I know what he will say to me when we are alone. What I don't know is how I will answer and whom I will have to answer to.

STRANGE VISITORS

Summer

Bears are coming down from the hills. They cross the river on narrow railway tracks, wade the shallow rapids near the island and are sighted on city streets. They are hungry. The summer has been hot and dusty, thunder in the evenings. Clouds roiling up slow and dark, growling, but no rain. And no berries to be found.

Sol watches and waits, but the bears come early in the morning, before he is even awake, or late at night, visiting him only in dreams.

His parents' voices seep under the door of his room at night like something unsettling rising from the cellar. Their voices rise like hawk and rabbit, wolf and deer, urgent and strange, so that he tosses, sweating, in his bed. He sleeps turned around, with his feet exposed at his headboard and his comforter pulled over his head to throw bad dreams off his scent.

His father walks with Sol on the first day of school. They stand waiting for the light, kitty-corner to the cemetery that dissolves into fog. Their side of the street has already burned through to sunlight.

"Do you think we'll see any bears over there?" Sol asks him, pointing to the cemetery.

"Maybe," he says. "You never know, but they'll be asleep now. Bears are nocturnal."

"I could bring wire from school and stretch it in front of our door."

"For what?"

"For nighttime. In case they come."

"Oh, you," Sol's father says, pushing the peak of his son's baseball cap over his eyes.

Night comes and with it, Sol's parents transform again. Sol's mother, who is often asleep when he comes home from school, paces the hallway. The bathroom door opens and closes, sending warm and cool air currents swirling above Sol's face in the dark. The stairs creak as she slips downstairs. After a while the groans and strange, gulping cries begin, then there is silence followed by the icy explosion of glass. Sol isn't sure if he is awake or asleep. His heart taps in his ears and the walls seem to sway as though they are breathing. He wants to call for his mother, but it has been a long time since he has done that.

Sol folds his face against the light in the hallway and stumbles downstairs, pulling at the sweaty waist of his pyjamas. She is lying on the couch with her head thrown back so far he can't see if it is still attached. Her bathrobe has slipped from her shoulders and knees. Her skin is pale and bluish, mottled like uncooked chicken. She looks cold. His father lies on top of her, half-dressed but strangely skewed, hurting them both.

Fall

"Here's one for your father and me, one for you and one for Jalna. I bet you miss her, Sol," the woman, Karen, says as she carefully lowers each lit candle to the surface of the lake. She lets each go with a tenderness that seems odd, given the frightening muscles of her arms. She is dark-haired, feet planted in a wide stride. It doesn't look right to see his father standing beside her. With his beard shaved off, he looks like a pale child, more like Sol's mother. Sol can't figure out what his father is doing here with this strong stranger.

"What an unusual name," she says to his father. "Jalna. I can't wait to meet her."

"The name was *her* idea. Girlhood readings, Mazo de la Roche, you know. She's like that. A bit fey," Sol's father says.

It has taken them the whole evening to make these floating candles from scraps of lumber, moss, bark and pine cones that drift slowly away toward the island. For a moment, one changes direction, floats close to shore, and Sol can see the pebbles on the bottom of the lake illuminated by a ring of strange light. Small fish follow, rising to kiss the floating candle as it moves away from land.

Then the three of them sit around a fire. Sol's father tells him, "She's been to the North Pole. She's taken her kayak up to the Bering Strait where the sun never sets. If you want, she could tell you about polar bears. Her tent was ripped open one morning by a polar bear."

"John," she says. "Don't you think that's a bit scary? Look, Sol, your candle is the only one left."

It flickers and shivers like a star, only closer and more precarious. A loon howls like a wolf, then its voice shakes with a crazed giggle somewhere out in the middle of darkness. She lifts her hands, cups her mouth and calls back. Sol's father tries, but breaks into laughter. Sol turns away from them and magically, the wail lifts from him, above the trees. The loon calls back. Sol looks out across the liquid darkness of the lake. The light of the last candle starts to beat like a small heart, drifting out near the island. It beats harder a few times, then goes out.

Sol arrives home and finds his mother sitting at the top of the stairs, her feet on the step, crying into her hands as though some invisible force won't let her pass. Jalna is home, not at the neighbours' as she usually is. She sits halfway up from the bottom, pointing at her mother's face, saying, "Mommy's sad."

His mother lifts her face from her hands, as if suddenly aware of where she is, and says, "It's not you, Jalna. You're a good girl. This comes from inside me."

"I come from inside you," Jalna says. "Right here." She pats her own belly.

His mother jumps a little when she catches sight of him.

She scuttles backward so all he can see are the bottoms of her bare feet.

"Is your father with you?" she whispers.

"Dad's outside. He wants to talk to you."

"No, not now. I have things to do. Jalna needs to ..." She doesn't finish.

Sol leads Jalna by the hand out the front door. She breaks away and runs to their father's car. After they have talked, he carries Jalna back and Sol follows behind. Sol is kissed on the top of the head as his father quietly opens the door and, without stepping over the threshold, places Jalna down inside.

"See you next weekend, kid," his father murmurs.

Sol knows his mother has melted away like mist. She is no longer at the top of the stairs. He will take a box of crackers out of the cupboard for Jalna, leave a little trail of crumbs so their mother can find her way back home.

The house grows narrower. There are rooms Sol can't enter anymore. The living room, where their mother used to sit in the afternoon sunlight to quilt, repels him. Across the room, squares of her most recent quilt lie disconnected in her basket, a needle piercing the skin-like surface. He used to play with the pieces she had cut, placing them within the squares of light on the floor formed by sun flooding through the windowpanes. His mother said, "Light and dark. We're going to contrast light and dark. Try it this way," and she knelt down beside him, moving the pieces around. At night, in his bed, he thinks about the pieces of her quilts, how they fit together, all those ragged shapes joining, until he falls asleep.

The woman his father has brought to their cottage for the second weekend in a row cuts across the water, the late western sun lighting up her wasp-yellow kayak. The paddle in her hands whirls like wings. For a moment she disappears behind an island. Sol stands ankle-deep in the cold lake. Fall is lighting matches of red and yellow in the highest branches. The trees lean into the lake, dry and crackling. Everything feels like it's about to go up in flames, but his feet are cold. Suddenly a whipping motion flings itself into the lake from the reeds to his right, a bolt of lightning zigzagging on the water across the red path of the sun.

"Look, Sol, a water snake," his father says. "Look at its speed! Pure muscle." Sol says nothing. He waits for it to hit its mark.

When light has fallen to the surface of the lake and all that's left is cold, tarnished silver, she slides her kayak up onto the wet sand, slips out of the cockpit. She hoists it up over one shoulder and steps soundlessly over rocks lining the shore.

"Wow," is all Sol's father says.

Sol lies upside down in his bed, but it doesn't work. The dreams come, even when he thinks he is awake. Their black cat, Panther, enters his room. But she is white and transparent. She walks right through the wood of the half-closed door, crosses near the foot of his bed and dissolves through the wall. On the way by, she flicks her tail and turns her face toward him, bored and nonchalant. Her eyes glow pink and Sol cries out when he sees the black net covering the sheen of her indifferent face.

His mother doesn't wake at first, but then she does, turning her face toward him. He sees that she, too, has been caught in the same net. Black threads cover her face framed by pale, dishevelled hair. Something trolling the river has caught them both.

"Turn your face away," he tells her as he climbs in beside her, taking his father's place. Sleep snips the threads, one by one, and he drifts far away.

Winter

Sol tells his father, "A million meteors hit earth every day. They fall onto our heads and houses, but they're only as big as a grain of sand. They're hitting our house right now."

His father has come home to shovel the first heavy snow and to take him skating. Sol tries to levitate from the snow angel he has made, but it doesn't work, no matter how hard he concentrates. His boot prints weigh down its wings and flowing gown.

"You don't need to worry about that. Things from outer space just bounce off our atmosphere and carry on their way," his father says as he flings a shovelful into the air.

"They're hitting our house right now," Sol tells him. He can't understand how his father can be so blind to the thousands of bright, diamond-sharp points he tosses over his shoulder.

Sol lies back with his face open to the burning blue, softened now and then by a passing cloud. One is the shape of an alligator. It twists and pulls and turns into a wolf. Every cloud is in the shape of something, perfect, but never predictable. Wolves, a snake, a hawk, then a bear. The snow obscures the house, the shrubs, his father, so that he is alone in a white cocoon under the blazing blue cold with its parade of shapes, slower than a cartoon, but much more mesmerizing.

"John, can you send Sol in? He needs to warm up before you take him," he hears his mother say, but he cannot move. Her voice is soft like it used to be, slightly teasing even when she doesn't mean it to be. The wind skitters little white mice across his face. They are weaving a crystal net, tying him down, dashing back and forth across his chest.

"He was here just a minute ago," his father says, his voice echoing between the garage door and the neighbours' house.

His mother's voice suddenly hardens, flies like a bird into the yard, swoops from place to place.

"Irresponsible! That's what you are! Sol," she calls. Then again, "Sol, are you there?"

But the mice have woven icy threads across his mouth.

She opens the car door. His father says, "You remember Karen from the cottage last fall?"

They skate along the canal, ice a dull grey, like the surface of an Etch A Sketch under the moonlight. Sol looks behind him at the luminous arcs, phosphorescent trails cut into the ice, following him. Karen has raced ahead, pumping her legs, one hand open behind her back as though she is going to grab him by the snowsuit and pull him along behind her. Sol and his father slow to a jagged march, then Sol sits in a snowbank.

"We'll never catch up, Sol."

"My back hurts," Sol says, leaning back, feeling the hard crust of icy snow dig into the little strip of neck exposed to the cold. They are on a stretch of canal that widens like a dark lake. Wind funnels between the canal's stone walls as if to extinguish the small globes of lights on their posts. They've skated so far, but the stars haven't budged. Then Sol sees a light shooting downward in a clear, quick arc.

"Dad, an arrow hit that building."

"A shooting star. That's one of your meteors."

"No. It was an arrow. I saw it."

In the restaurant, the warm, spicy smell hits Sol in the face like steam. The present Karen has given him still lies on top of the torn wrapping paper.

"I know Christmas is over," she says, "but here's a blank notebook for your field observations. Your dad and I keep notes in one just like it. You can take it with you when we go on adventures."

"He's too young, Karen. I told you."

"He's a smart boy, like his father," she says, smiling in a way that gives Sol an unpleasant tickle in his stomach.

Sol turns the coiled book in his hands. He opens it to the first page and carefully writes with his father's pen: MOM.

Beneath it, he draws his mother, a teetering stick figure with hands as large as suns, beaming rays in all directions. Karen leans back, away from him, quiet, before she says, "OK."

Sol is occupied with his new notebook. Like the wake from a small motorboat, their voices turn toward him and away, rising and falling, until settling into a calm, remote line of adult conversation. He writes carefully, even though his letters are large and shaky. The waiter brings them little stuffed triangles, his brown hands appearing even darker against the white tablecloth. Sol wants to touch them. Instead, he holds up the notebook.

But Karen grabs the book from his hands, saying, "Sol, that's not nice, what you've written. It's not."

"Wait a minute, Karen. He's only six."

"People are sensitive. Sol, he's from India. This is a vegetarian restaurant. Do you know what a vegetarian is?"

"It's innocent enough. Let him have the book," his father says.

"Vegetarians don't eat meat. We don't hurt animals."

Sol's mouth burns from the strange food that smells so sweet, but then fills his eyes with tears. He knows they are watching him as he draws a picture beneath the words, a clump with whiskers and a snakey line trailing behind. He knows Karen will not stop him again. His father watches her the same way she watches Sol. As the waiter clears away their three little plates, he lifts the book and turns it outward:

ETE

THE RAT

This time, the waiter sees the message Sol is passing him and chuckles, his eyes sparkling in the candlelight. Karen and his father are not looking at each other.

When the waiter brings more wine, Sol holds up his book again. He is free to do as he wishes. He has added a jagged horizon and a moon.

The waiter laughs out loud and puts his warm, brown hand on Sol's head. Sol writes:

THAN
KYOU

All the way home in the back seat, Sol practises the scheming laugh of the loon. He cups his mouth and lets his voice soar high above the sound of the car, the sound of the city, sound so pure it silences their conversation in the front seat.

Sol tells his mother he saw an arrow in the sky, that it didn't hit anybody, just a building.

"What does it feel like when you're hit with Cupid's arrow?" he asks her.

She looks at him and pulls him close, breathes into his hair still damp from the bath and whispers, "It hurts." Then she laughs.

Spring

Sol says to his mother as they walk home from school, "I'm lucky. Nobody else at school is going to see the eclipse."

"You certainly are," she says. "Did you know we named you after the sun? 'Sol' means 'sun.' Because it was a beautiful day when you were born."

When he saw her waiting in the school yard holding Jalna's hand, he started to jiggle his knees with excitement. She is wearing pale blue, washed out below the intense cool blue sky of spring. Other mothers nearby are still earthen in their winter clothes. His mother stands apart, the colour of early mornings in summer, as though she has missed all the cold seasons in between. Now she is standing, thin and upright, shimmering in her light dress.

"Do you know what an eclipse is?" she asks him.

"It's when it gets dark in the middle of the day."

"That's it. The school wants to keep you in, but we can watch from home. It's a special day and you shouldn't miss it."

He stays close to his mother as they cross the busy street at the crosswalk. The cars stop in both directions when she stretches out her arm and he feels her power strengthening like a force field all around him. Jalna asks, "Can I see the clips, too?"

"If you don't get too tired. It's during your nap time." The tulips in the cemetery throb vivid red.

Sol and his mother sit side by side on the cool concrete of the front step facing the huge maple in their yard. Jalna, who asked over and over, "Is it now?" sleeps inside on the couch with her striped blanket pulled up close to her face, perfuming the air with peace.

"I know just the thing for you. I'll make you a quilt of the eclipse for your next birthday, each square a different phase. You can sleep under the sun, even at night," his mother says, hugging him suddenly.

His mother's arm around him is warm and he moves in closer to her body as the intense blue of the sky gradually drains to a remote violet, as though outer space in all its blackness has found a hairline fracture where it can seep in. The tree before them stops shaking its tiny leaves, darkens and broods.

They sit for a long time, looking out at gloom. He inhales a shallow, cautious breath, and the air does feel different, as though some of the airless void beyond the world has pressed in closer.

Then, almost imperceptibly, light returns and spring arrives, in a matter of minutes.

A BOX FULL OF WIND

K it tells me the goats at the cooperative farm where she spent the summer will never be slaughtered. The goats are raised for their milk, which is turned into soap, and for their silky coats, spun into the wool sold at Kit's parents' antique and curio shop.

Kit came back so brown that, with her fine white-blond hair, she looks like a photonegative of herself. Her body has swollen into curves. She says the farm is in the hills north of here and I imagine her lying down and taking on their shape against the sky. It's as though her breasts and hips have been witched out of her by a willow stick. Her blood, too, has jumped through her skin in an explosion of blemishes.

She seems quieter somehow, even though she's taken up wearing the outlandish clothes sold at her parents' shop. When winter arrives, she wears a brown ankle-length maxicoat from the Sixties, lined and trimmed with fake Persian lamb, and soft, grey leather boots that end above her knees. She pulls them on like stockings and they slip down and wrinkle elephant-like at the knees and ankles. A thin band of skin below her short skirt attracts looks from passing men in the hotel lobby. She doesn't seem to notice.

Maybe her boots are the reason we no longer run up and down the hallways. Instead, we loiter on one of the silk sofas in the lobby before we take the bus home from what was supposed to be our class at the School of Art. On the afternoons devoted to still life, we slip over here to the hotel instead, explore floors of mirror-ended halls, throw pennies in the fountain and wish for our lives to begin.

Kit nudges me so I look at a woman in a rose-coloured coat, too tight for her age. Her hand balances discreetly on a man's sleeve.

"She's checking into a hotel at two o'clock in the afternoon when she's supposed to be on her way to a funeral in Montreal," Kit says.

"What about her?" I point to a sad, beige woman carrying a canvas suitcase.

"The most desperate kind. She flew here from Winnipeg, somewhere flat and boring, and he won't even show up because he's home borrowing a cup of sugar from the neighbour's wife," Kit says.

Kit knows about such things. Her parents take meditation classes, go on weekend encounters. I've seen them sitting cross-legged on the floor in candlelight, their hands held in the laps of strangers, moaning softly in unison, "Oooohhmmm," like wind through telephone wires. Her mother wears bell-bottom pants winter and summer, her belly button squinting out from under short muslin tops.

Kit's mother turns toward us as we come through the

kitchen door. Something about the way she swings her long red hair promises a warmth and vitality I don't find in my own mother, yet her sharp profile and small feral mouth catch me by surprise. She smiles with human teeth and says, "Hey, there. Where've *you* been?"

"Still life class. Remember?" Kit balances on one foot to pull her boot off by the baggy stuff at the ankle.

"Oh, yeah. Hector's here from the farm. He's staying over tonight. Why don't you show him your work? Maybe he could give you some pointers."

"I left it there to dry," Kit says, then decides to humour her. "Besides, it's already the most brilliant wrinkled eggplant ever put to paper. Just at the point of rotting. If you're good, you'll get it for Mother's Day."

She laughs, but I can see her uncertainty before she turns to me.

"Did you paint the same still life, Annie?"

I pause, dumbstruck, and Kit jumps in to save me. "No. She painted kumquats. A whole bowl of them. Annie's going to stay tonight. OK?"

This is news to me, but my parents won't mind. My father is likely just rising from his long drunken nap on the den floor, scowling, suddenly sober and none too happy about it, and my mother is probably gathering up her crossword puzzles to take to her room for the night. One call and I'm free.

"I don't even know what kumquats look like," I say.

"Neither do I. Green and horny?" she says and we burst into hysterical laughter. I trail Kit into the living room, looking around quickly to see what has changed since the last time I was here. Kit's house is always in flux. Furniture changes week to week, depending on what her parents move into the shop. They comb flea markets, auctions, estate sales for furniture, paintings, vintage clothes, tablecloths, anything funky. The only constant is a blue-and-white covered vase on the mantle.

"Meet my baby brother," Kit said, waving her arm toward the mantle, the first time she led me through the living room. "He used to be a redhead like my mom, but now he's ash-blond."

Even for Kit, this was pushing it. She must have noticed I didn't laugh like I usually did at her bad jokes. Neither of us mentioned the vase again, although I slip a glance at it each time we pass.

The only other time she mentioned her brother, we were in the kitchen, and I was reaching for a brownie.

"That stuff tastes like cow feed," she said, pulling the pan out of reach. "Hash brownies, you know?" Before I had a chance to hide it, she caught the embarrassment on my face. She knew it wasn't because she stopped me. We were always raiding each other's kitchens.

"My dad used to be a lawyer before Aidan died. Three-piece suit in the morning and everything. You'd never know it now."

"What happened to him?" I asked, scraping dried icing off the countertop. "Your brother, I mean."

"Crib death. It was nobody's fault," she said.

Today, a large wooden box the shape of an oversized coffin rests on huge carved legs, taking up half the living room floor. We have to walk around it, but the musty smell is too alluring. Kit moves a heavy green polished rock from the top of it and places it on a pine sideboard.

"Another of Hector's brilliant creations. He keeps giving us this junk for the shop. He says it's aboriginal art." Kit laughs. "He claims he's one-eighth Mohawk."

She turns back to the wooden box, lifts the flap with both arms straining against the weight and peers inside. She braces the lid, flips another smaller lid up and back.

"It's a table grand piano. You've probably never seen one before. They went out of fashion a hundred years ago. People used to eat off them when company came."

There's a space big enough to climb inside, a dark interior snarled with coils of tarnished metal strings. Below me are yellow teeth, gaps where some are missing, others permanently depressed as if by some invisible giant. Kit pokes at the keyboard. Some click dull, others, even when hit hard, are silent. Only a few keys strike a hollow out-of-tune note, a box full of wind, trapped for a hundred years.

"My dad and Hector are going to strip it, take the insides out and seal it. They'll sell it for a lot of money."

I associate her father with only two things: the smell of smouldering hay and the sound of his nighttime reconstructions, the thumps and scrapings, the screech of legs on their basement floor. They are furtive sounds, sounds of making illegal money, moving piles of it from one part of the house to another, though what her father does is legal enough. It's just that smell drifting up the stairs that's not. I never let on I notice.

"C'mon. Let's call somebody," Kit says.

We call Alison, but she isn't home. Then, on an impulse, we call girls we know who aren't actually our friends. If their parents answer, we hang up immediately, but when we are lucky enough to hear a voice we know, querulous, "Hello? Is anybody there? Hell-ooo?" we crowd closer to the phone, stifling an uproar. We wait it out until one of us snorts, then we slam down the phone as fits of laughter overtake us.

Kit says, "Let's see how long we can keep them on the phone."

Our record is eight minutes. We call restaurants and ask elaborate questions about their menus, pretend to misunderstand directions for pick-up. An all-night delicatessen puts us on hold for nine minutes, but we decide that doesn't count.

We branch out, dial numbers we make up. Kit reaches an older woman who speaks something like Russian, all spitting, angry syllables. I don't even need to put my ear against the receiver to hear her yell as Kit's pitch to sell dog food comes to an abrupt end.

"I had to put her out of her misery," Kit says as she hangs up. "This is too easy. Let's make a rule. We're not allowed to tell a lie."

Suddenly there is a keening howl from somewhere far off. It's a cry of pain, the sound of flesh separating from spirit. It rumbles, veers through the lower register and rises to a falsetto howl.

Kit stands tall, her back against the wall, bracing for the unexpected. She reaches across and quietly opens the door.

"It's coming from the living room. Is it your mother?" I whisper to Kit, imagining her sylph of a mother losing her composure, lying prostrate below the mantle that holds the blue-and-white vase.

"No, stupid," Kit says and strides out of the room.

All we see at first is the grey-and-white head of a small cat, neck stretched, eyes two narrow slits. The sick crooning continues as we inch around the corner. The cat's body is flat against the frayed Oriental rug, its tail high in the air, its spine a hard arc. Connected to the raised backside of the cat is a man's foot in a coarse wool sock. He sits on a spindly Queen Anne's chair in the dark living room. He's no one I've ever seen before. I'd have remembered the gaunt bones of his face above the blur of his beard, the two sandy-coloured braids tight behind his ears. He turns his sleepy, blue eyes toward us and grins.

"Where did the cat come from?" Kit asks.

"The front yard. I heard her yowling and saved her from being raped," he says. "The toms had her cornered."

"And what are you going to do with her?"

"Maybe I'll keep her. Maybe I'll leave her here for you to remember me by when I'm gone. Who's this?" he asks, glancing my way. I look down at my chest. I always thought nobody noticed how flat I am, but he does, and he thinks it's funny.

"Just a friend," Kit says. "She's staying over."

"Aren't you a little old for sleepovers? You never know what trouble you'll get yourself into," he says, winking, then focusing on the wailing cat again. He's rubbing his toes in rhythmic circles around her back end as she pushes against his foot, crooning.

"That's disgusting," Kit says.

"Oh, you're a sweet little kitten, aren't you. Yes, I know what it's like. Oh, yes, just stay right here. Oh yes," he says. "You love it, don't you? You love it."

"Stop it," Kit says.

He lifts his blue eyes, half-closed, teasing her.

"I don't hear her complaining. Who's going to argue with millions of years of evolution? When she's ready, she's ready. Maybe I'll keep her in my bed tonight to keep me warm. What do you think about that?"

Kit turns and walks out. I follow her back to her room.

"Hector's a pervert," she says.

She sits on her bed, brooding, then swings her feet up, crosses them in front of her, leans back on her hands. She lifts her chin, looking at the ceiling, and laughs from the back of her throat. If she read my mind, she'd hear what my parents say behind her back.

"Where were we? Oh, yeah, if we call somebody, we can't lie." She thinks a little and grins.

"You remember that teacher who got into trouble? Mr. Maharry, remember? He was caught screwing around with that crazy girl in Grade 13? Let's call him," Kit says.

"How do you know his name? We weren't even in high school when that happened."

She stretches her legs out in front of her, tilts her head to one side.

"I make it my business. There are girls around who

knew her. She told them sometimes they used to do it in the bathroom stalls."

"Sitting down? How could they do it sitting down?" I ask.

"You really can be dumb sometimes. Standing up in the boys' washroom. Boys never use the stalls unless they're desperate. No one would see anything but two feet turned around the wrong way."

"Wouldn't they be facing forward?"

"No. The guy has to hold the girl up over the toilet. She'd have her legs around his waist, and if he doesn't fall down when he comes, who would know she's there?"

This is too technical for me; I have a hard time picturing it.

"How will we find him?" I say, looking for a way out.

"How many Maharrys do you think there are?" she says.

We both howl with laughter when we find his name in the phone book. There are only two Maharrys: E. Maharry and Duke Maharry.

"*Duke. Duke* Maharry. It's got to be him with a name like that," Kit says. "Do you like ma harry thing?"

"I don't know, Kit."

"You don't like ma harry thing. I'm a gonna cry." Then she says, "You time me. You can just listen."

She plugs the phone from her parents' room into the jack in the hall, carefully closing the door on the cord and handing me the extra phone.

The man's voice is boozy, thick and sleepy at first. I recognize the rough growl of someone awakened from a drunken sleep.

"Hello," he says, as though he knows in advance he'll be disappointed.

"Hi," Kit says. "How are you tonight?"

"I don't want to buy anything."

"Sure, but I'm not selling. That's not why I called."

"So?" he says.

"So," she says. Then a pause.

"What do you want?" he asks, anger in his voice.

"Just want to talk." Another pause.

"Who is this?" His voice has suddenly thinned, a slight quavering in the upper register.

"Don't you know?"

"Tell me." Something between apprehension and eagerness. "It can't be, after all this time."

"Yes, it is. It's me."

"Meredith." Heavy, heartfelt, a statement. "Meredith, is that you?"

Kit looks over at me, mouthing the words, "Remember the rule," and says nothing.

"I knew sooner or later you'd call. Here you are. God, Meredith, why now? Do you have any idea what's happened?"

"No."

"Everything fell apart. Everything."

"I'm sorry," Kit says.

"Sorry. *Now* you're sorry. Where the hell were you? I lost my job. Beth went to the principal. She told them I wasn't fit to teach and it was true. I wasn't. They have rules about this sort of thing. I didn't deny it, but if you'd been around, they could have seen for themselves."

Kit is pointing at her watch and lifts a finger to mark the passing of a minute.

"I wondered where you were. I remember the stories you told me about how you used to trick your mother."

"I'm not that far away now," Kit says.

"You might as well have been in Timbuktu. Beth and I split up, you know. We lost the house. My father hangs up on me. Beth hangs up on me. I've got the right to see Christine, but what's the point? She's old enough to hang up on me, too."

"I didn't know."

"It wouldn't have been so bad if you'd been here. What happened?"

"Oh, you know, this and that. Nothing special."

"I'll bet. You always did like to live dangerously. I suppose there have been men. Lots of them."

"Not many," Kit says.

"Then again, maybe you joined a convent, shaved off all your beautiful hair. You like to surprise people, don't you?"

"Yeah, I guess I do."

"You sound different." He pauses. "Not as I remember you."

"How do you remember me?"

"The first time I saw you, the sun slanting through the window onto that fiery hair of yours. You knew, didn't you, you knew what you were going to do to me."

"No, I didn't know a thing."

"I wasn't the first. I knew that much. Whenever I walk by a broom closet and catch the smell of industrial cleaner, I remember, and I feel shaky for the rest of the day."

"Did you mind?" Kit asks.

He pauses for a minute, then says, "Not then."

"But now?"

"Now I'm on my own. I've got to tell the truth; it's been rough. And Beth, when I see her, has this tense white line just above her brow. *I* put it there."

I watch Kit. She's lying on the bed, completely unmoved. She grins at me with her eyebrows raised. She mouths, "Poor him."

"Hang up," I mouth back at her. I make the motions of putting down the receiver with my other hand.

"Why do men do such stupid things?" he asks.

"Girls do stupid things, too," she says and for the first time she looks a little tired.

"Is that how you think of me now, Meredith? Just a stupid thing you did once?" He's angry, so it comes out quickly. "You weren't throwing anything away as far as I could tell." He pauses, then says, "It's strange, I've been thinking about you. The things I didn't know about you, and then you call."

He stops, but Kit seems to know he's not finished. She waits, her lower lip under her front teeth.

"That time we slept together, the only time we had a whole night," he says. "You remember that motel near Otter Lake? You kicked and thrashed all night. Every time I settled you down, you would start again. Your eyes were open, but you weren't awake. I've thought about that since. I never asked what was bothering you."

Kit doesn't say anything. He's waiting for something and whatever it is terrifies him.

"What do you do now, for a living?" she says, changing the subject. He welcomes the diversion.

"You'll laugh. I hate to tell you, but I was really desperate. All I'd ever done was teach."

"I won't laugh," Kit says.

"I sell insurance, on commission. It's like teaching, in a way. I do a lot of talking."

She says nothing.

"So, should we reminisce about the good times? God, you were one wild girl. Remember when you faked appendicitis so I'd have to take you to the hospital?"

He's laughing, but it sounds more like gasping. A fish out of water. "I was more worried about being arrested for indecent exposure than being caught by Beth." He stops, then says, "It felt like that, when it finally happened. I wish it could have been different, the way she found out. More dignified, but that's not your style, is it?"

"I wouldn't know about that," Kit says, looking over at me and winking.

"*I* know."

"People change. You've changed."

"What choice was there?"

"I'm here," she says.

"No. You can't be."

"Yes, I am," Kit says emphatically. "I'm really here."

"Did you just get in?"

"I've been here for a while, but I'm glad we finally connected."

"Have you been trying to reach me?"

"Just tonight. Why don't we meet ..." Kit says, pausing.

I'm slashing the air with my hand, mouthing, "No more, no more."

"Are you close to downtown? How about meeting for a drink? At The Pump. Hey, you're over nineteen now. You're legal. Finally," he says.

"Great!" Kit says.

"In an hour?"

"Sure. An hour's fine."

"I want to hear everything, all your adventures, no matter how crazy."

And then he's gone. Kit gently puts down the phone, puts her hand over her mouth.

"Fifteen minutes and thirty-five seconds. That's an all-time record," she says.

"Kit, you should call him back before he leaves," I say.

"That's what he gets," Kit says.

"It's not funny. He'll be all alone."

"Tough," Kit says and flings herself back on her pillow.

Kit has given me her bed and every time I toss, I see her curled up tight below me on the floor, her blond hair sheltering her shoulders, her hands and arms folded up like little wings, tight under her chin. I dream restlessly, endlessly, of echoing hallways, of bright lights and escalators that move upward into clouds. I hear the wail of a baby far off and find myself suddenly awake. I turn, but Kit is no longer there on the floor beside me.

I am not surprised that she is gone. Her blankets and sheets have been swirled into stiff, awkward shapes by turbulent wind. She is out there somewhere, buffeted, and drifting as I am between dreams and waking, I know with the logic of dreams where she is. She is in the cavity of the table grand piano. The yellow keys and broken strings have been removed. The lid has been closed forever. Her brother is on the mantle in his vase and she is in the table grand. Her cry, if there is one, circles around where no one can hear.

SILENT SISTER

J anice stands at the Champlain lookout and squints against the sun glinting off the silver channel far below. Her sister, Lotus, disappeared into that river last winter. She still can't fathom it. Lotus drifting, eddying, or snagged on the rocky river bottom are impossible images, only real when they float in the dark above her bed like holograms when she can't sleep. Words like "grief" or "anger" cannot capture the waste of her sister's life, but this failure to fathom can.

Lotus' body has never been found. Her parents disagree about what actually happened to her. When her body hadn't surfaced in May, along with the other suicides and accident victims, her family grew more rancorous. The police stopped returning their phone calls. A neighbour told Janice's mother about an island downriver where bodies that have somehow slipped through the grates near the paper mill are snagged by tree roots. Bones are found there years after people go missing. Out of their jurisdiction, the police say. Janice is willing to search for a bleached tibia, a rounded skull. Would she even recognize her sister? But no one seems to know where this island might be.

Janice came here, on Thanksgiving Sunday, to this lookout high on the Eardly Escarpment, by chance. She drove over the bridge, away from the downtown market with its decorative gourds, orange as chemical fires, its dried flowers, to the Gatineau Parkway. She is one of the last visitors of the season. Only one other car is in the lot, with no occupants in sight. She presses her hands against the cold rock of the curving stone wall and looks across the lowlands: orderly farms and straight country roads, the river glistening poisonous grey, heavy as mercury, full of bays and islands invisible from lower ground. She cannot see the buildings or smoke stacks of the paper mill.

Next to Janice's right hand, embedded in rock, is a copper arrow pointing out into windy space. Dunrobin, nine miles. She peers, but can't see any sign of human habitation. Beside her left hand, another arrow points in a different direction: Buckingham, twenty-four miles. Moving along the wall, she finds scarred indentations where copper arrows once bolted onto rock have been removed.

She descends the stone stairs, lifting the brochure *Interpretation of the Champlain Trail* from beneath a clear plastic trap door. She appreciates the clarity of the brochure, the bullets in point form outlining areas to be covered: start and finish, time required, length, change of elevation, terrain and a neat map, simple as a comic book, of the trail she will follow. She feels she is in safe hands and moves toward the first of the EIGHT POINTS OF INTEREST.

She stood here early last summer. 1. THE RED OAKS OF THE ESCARPMENT, but she hadn't noticed the sturdy trees stunted by wind. All she remembers of her June scurry around part of this trail is her awkward platform shoes and Charles Danson's squared shoulders as he walked ahead of her. She remembers her hunger, like a weakness.

Earlier that day, he had talked with the paper mill's biologist. Already he was an expert on mercury contamination, had assimilated and reinterpreted all the research she had done for him, late at night in the library. She was so absorbed in what she was reading she had almost forgotten him. She read of Minimata Bay in Japan, where a chemical company had dumped its effluent into a bog. Mercury sank to the bottom and was converted by the bacteria in the mud from inorganic to organic methyl mercury, entering the food chain through microscopic underwater life, increasing in concentration and toxicity as it accumulated in the organs of larger hosts. It was this one detail, one small link in this chain of creation, that he had isolated for his argument.

"You didn't, at any time, dump methyl mercury. The bacteria is polluting this river, not you," he said to the mill's biologist. He stood up, satisfied. She made notes, adding to the hundreds of pages of research she had already conducted, her writing growing spiky with agitation. It was hard to separate what she learned from what she felt. An almost imperceptible tingling around the lips, in the fingertips and toes, tunnel vision. She had read of the effects: body movement would become uncoordinated, blindness would set in before delirium, coma, death. The Japanese living in

Minimata Bay had at first called it "dancing cat disease" because their cats, fed on the entrails of fish, were the first affected. Cats staggered, squealed, slobbered and lurched recklessly about, then threw themselves into the sea or crashed against walls before dropping dead.

After they left the paper mill, she drove him along the parkway into the Gatineau Hills. He raised his eyes as she parked at the lookout, smiled and said, "Janice, what do you have in mind?" But he took his time. It was near the end of their affair.

It bothers her now that she felt nothing for Lotus that day even though she had disappeared only a few months earlier. Her misery had been all about him, about Charles Danson. When she thinks of him, it is always by both his names. Perhaps because he appears that way in newspapers. She hears Lotus' voice goading her, "Charles Danson, defender of polluters, money-grubbers, sleazy politicians." But all Lotus had ever said after she had seen them together in a tiny downtown park was, "Careful." Her silence had been uncharacteristic.

Now Janice moves into a wide hollow of stone, finds the wooden post marked 2. FAULTS AND HOLLOWS and reads the description: a ravine formed by surface waters flowing through a crack in the bedrock. Whose fault was it finally that her relationship with Lotus eroded? Who created this wide, stony gulf between them? Lotus had always seemed so buoyant and certain. She would master a skill, then Janice would too, shaky at first, but determined.

The two of them had gone to wilderness survival camp the summer their parents toured Italy. The camp was Lotus' idea: the long, sweltering hikes, nights humming with insects, water heated over a fire smelling musky as animal breath. They spent a night together far from the others, eating only what they could find. Lotus caught frogs in the shallows of the reedy lake, killed them quickly with a knife. Janice reeled at the surprising sight of red blood. She couldn't eat the legs, browned and sizzling, cooked with wild mushrooms. She lifted to her mouth the slippery white bulbs of bulrushes, but their faint oniony smell made her feel sick.

"You'll be weak by morning. It's a long walk back," Lotus said.

"I can't. I just can't," Janice admitted, ashamed. "How can you eat them after you've killed them?"

Lotus sat back, holding the stick she was using to stir. "It's the only honest way," she said.

When night fell, Lotus tried to calm her by pointing out constellations in her hushed, quick voice.

"You're seeing light that left those stars years ago," she said. "Even the sun's light has to travel to us. It will only last four million more years. But we won't know the sun's gone till eight minutes after it's over."

"Don't be mean. You're scaring me on purpose."

"It's OK. Really. Look at your hand. The atoms in your body come from dead stars. Did you know that? You wouldn't be here if it weren't for dead stars." She sat closer to Janice on the dewy grass, put her arm around her, and pulled her closer. Lotus' body was already softly formed, a woman's body, the only warmth anywhere in that forlorn forest next to a lake throbbing with frogs, under a dizzying sky full of stars she couldn't trust.

They hadn't seen each other much in recent years, not since Lotus turned up in the hallway of Janice's apartment building. Janice was tired from long hours in the law library. Lotus was waiting for her, black hair brittle from the chemicals she took, her bones thin as a switchblade, looking for a fight.

"It's a lot of work being the enemy of women, isn't it?"

"You mean studying law?"

"If we had a rape law as strong as our extortion law, we'd be getting somewhere," Lotus said.

"I'm going to bed now," Janice said, turning away.

"Intimidation, fear, an implied threat. Sound familiar?" Lotus backed her into a corner.

Janice slid sideways and walked away, exhausted.

Lotus was the one their father had assumed had the true legal mind. After dinner, Lotus went with him to his study, spent evenings poring over his books as he patiently explained precedents. Janice could hear their murmuring from the kitchen. Only her mother, Rose, sat with Janice over dessert, solicitous, claiming her with a wry, direct smile. Janice knew that her father had chosen Lotus. He had cultivated Lotus' energy, kept her informed, got her a summer job when she was in her teens typing papers for his law firm, Danson & Marshall.

Charles Danson had mentioned Lotus once at the beginning of their affair, as they sat in his Jaguar in a city park, watching a teenaged girl throw a Frisbee for a large black dog.

"What's wrong with your sister? Your father had such high hopes for her."

"You know Lotus?"

"Sure, she worked for us. I see her on the streets. Hard to miss with those dogs trailing her everywhere. Her looks have gone to hell."

"She's ill. She's up and down."

"Imagine wasting a mind like that. She did some research for me once or twice. Very clever. She was a natural for law. She had a quick tongue," he said. "Now she looks like a tubercular from the last century, an Emily Brontë character. The glamorous tragedy, the dogs, the wild black hair, you know the type."

"She isn't a *type*. She's my sister, for God's sake."

"She fell in love with her own plight and threw away her future to prove it."

Janice was stung by his callousness.

His words rang in her head when she was alone. How much of it was obsession, how much of it was doing her job better than anyone else, she couldn't tell. She grew restless when she was apart from him, turned to books to ferret out details he might use. It was a habit that calmed her. She looked up tuberculosis, an illness of starved fevers and delirium. She read the Brontës, Thomas Mann. She saw Lotus striding across the moors followed by dogs, addicted to the rarefied mountain air of the sanatorium. She read about patients who heated their thermometers on sunny windowsills, throwing themselves into rivers to provoke pneumonia, so determined were they not to leave. Their doctors would catch some of them with a *silent sister*, a mercury thermometer without gradations that only the staff could read accurately.

Now, as she walks the trail, Janice looks at the river on her left, shiny hot even though the air is cool. Her sister's body, she tells herself, is part of that slow column of mercury, part of the current beneath the glowing surface. Her sister's fingers scrape sludge from the river bottom. Her sister's mouth fills with pulp from the mill upriver. Her once skeletal body bloats with heavy metals, a weather balloon drifting through chemical clouds that blossom from the ends of drainpipes planted deep in the river floor.

She feels suddenly light-headed, turns her face away from the wind. She looks down at the booklet in her hands, then spots 3. IRONWOOD ahead on her right. Just trees, straight, narrow and tough. "The reputation of the Ironwood is well deserved; its wood is almost impossible to split!" Janice reads, leaning all her weight against the tree. It doesn't sway, doesn't respond to her presence.

Her parents received a photograph in the mail. It was from the front page of the *Globe and Mail* last June. A young woman was being removed from a protest site at Clayoquot Sound. It took three police officers to carry her: two holding her hands, her face tipped back, exposing a thin, white neck; and one holding her legs slightly apart. It could have been Lotus. There was the same tense line of neck, the familiar sandals, thick-soled, with treads like snow tires. A pale dog, mouth wide and snarling, blurred the corner of the photograph. Her father called the paper and managed to trace the photographer. He even checked the names of protesters arrested that day. Finally, the woman in the photo was identified. She was a student at Simon Fraser, alive and well.

The trail emerges from the sparse forest clinging to the rocky slopes of the escarpment, crosses a stream and leads her once again to the edge. She follows wooden stairs down to a small lookout perched over the precipice. The wind sighs through the chicken wire secured over the spaces between wooden rails. The river hasn't changed in perspective even though she's been walking for half an hour. The same islands and bays, the same thick current moving across her field of vision. She looks up and her heart jumps. A figure flies silently on wind currents, level with her, angling out toward the river. The legs of the figure hang down between rigid wings, as though half swallowed by a bird of prey. It is a hang glider, the shape of a pterodactyl, a preancestral memory.

She couldn't help it. She was fascinated by his slightly florid face, his eyes, a surprisingly weak blue. Charles Danson took her up in his plane to show her how peaceful it was in the sky, how everything below was orderly and graceful. He glided, let the currents carry him. She expected peace, maybe a spiritual vision, but instead he stalled the engines, jerked the plane into dives and sudden recoveries. She was terrified.

Lotus would have been fierce enough to dive off the edge of this escarpment, or out of his plane, plummeting into air. Janice remembers being at a public swimming pool with Lotus the first time she starved herself in her teens. Over and over, Lotus lined up to swing on a rope across the deep end. She was shivering, a translucent blue, her stomach caved in under her ribs, on the deck with children half her height. She lifted her skeletal body high and swung out over the deep, sleepy water, dropping into the pool perfectly straight. Each time, she held the bones of her legs more rigid, her toes pointed. Children's eyes were drawn to her; it was obvious they were frightened. There was no pleasure in it for Lotus, either; her face was pallid, rapt. For hours, dropping into the water toes first, disappearing with barely a ring of ripples until the lifeguard approached her and said, "Enough is enough." The same thing her father said after paying for five sessions with a psychologist, during which she sat in silence.

The trail turns inland now, away from the view of the river, relaxes and slows through sparse, rocky forest where the only real colour is the deep green of moss pillowing on the ground, on the dark sides of tree trunks. Thick shrubby trees shelter her from the wind, the same juniper-like hedges along her parents' street.

The last time she saw Lotus was Thanksgiving, the air after rain full of this same dense fragrance. When she arrived at her parents' house, she was shocked by how thin

Lotus had become again. Her dark eyes were like puncture wounds in the whiteness of her face.

They stood together at the counter, preparing a salad. Lotus snipped lettuce with scissors. She was restless, kept getting up to open the kitchen door to the laneway, where her two dogs were waiting for her, whimpering. Every time she closed the door, they heard a dog's nails scratching on glass.

Their mother said, "Do you have to bring those dogs everywhere you go?"

"If you don't want them to scratch, you have to let them in," Lotus said.

"I told you last time. I don't want dogs in here. They're not very well trained."

"I'm not very well trained and you let me in."

"Lotus, they're only dogs."

"We're all only bitches, Mother."

Rose walked out of the room. She never fought with Lotus.

Lotus didn't eat much at dinner. She didn't sit long enough. Janice whispered, "Is she starving herself again?" but their mother pretended she hadn't heard.

Strangely enough, Lotus joined them for dessert, dissecting a slice of angel food cake as she turned her fierce eyes on their father. She demanded to know if he had signed the organ donor card on his driver's licence.

"So, have you given your body to science?"

"What is the point of this?" he said, looking up from his own empty plate. He had long since given up, understood that all she intended was parody.

"Come on. What's the difference? A good provider like you. Why not give the whole thing to science?"

"You look to yourself for a change. Look at your own body. When you're a paragon of good health, maybe someone will listen to you."

"Simmer down. Such overt emotionalism. I'm surprised at you letting an argument slip away from you like that," Lotus said with a quick, smug smile.

"Is that what this is about, the waste of your life? Winning an argument? Well you choose your forum and you play by the *rules*."

Lotus lifted the ends of her long hair and studied them, found a split end, peeled it apart with her fingernails.

Janice isn't sure, after all, if she wants to hear Lotus' voice ringing so clearly in her head. Her presence had been so palpable, a mist of icy chemical making them all take shallow breaths when they sensed she was particularly on edge. She had never allowed her body one ounce of softness. She was jutting bones, her hair in points, a display of thin blades.

Janice reaches 4. SUGAR MAPLE FOREST. This is the mythical forest of fairy tales; a forest of sweetness locked deep inside, just a scent wafting from tree to tree.

Lotus and Janice left their parents' house that night at the same time. They sat on the steps in the laneway as Lotus' dogs jumped all over her.

"What are their names?" Janice asked.

"Who knows?"

"Don't they answer to you?"

"This one," Lotus said, taking the small, light-brown head in her hands, "came out of nowhere. I caught her tipping over trash cans and fell in love for the first time. Sometimes I call her Precious.

"Or Fou Fou," Janice added and they laughed softly, their heads close for the first time in years.

"*Mon Cherie*. But really, look at her eyes. Who knows what she's been through? I could try every word in the language and not find just the one she answers to. Sometimes I just call her Lotus. After all, it's not really my name."

"Better than Lois. I did you a favour. And him?"

"Bones."

Lotus reached down and picked up a small white pebble, rolled it between her fingers.

"Are you all right?" Janice said.

"All right. Sure."

"You're so thin. Why can't you eat?"

Janice had never been so direct. Her heart was pounding. Lotus kept her face turned away. She let the silence grow until Janice couldn't bear it.

"I'm going by your place. Do you want a ride?"

"Ugh. In your coffin on wheels? You drivers should be buried in them before you do any more harm."

Janice walked alone to her car. She was stung by the sudden attack. Through the rearview mirror, she could barely make out the slight outline of her sister slipping away as the dogs swarmed behind her in the dark.

She has only two more stops before the trail loops back out to the parking lot. She feels a panic rising in her throat. She crosses a marshy section on a boardwalk, starts to climb again, looking urgently for the next post. It isn't to be found. She sweeps through tall fiddlehead ferns, still electric green, and her boot thuds against concrete. She's found the base, but the post has vanished. She looks in her brochure to see what she's missing. 5. THE TATTLE-TALES. "Plants are choosy about where they grow," it starts, and explains tricks for discovering clues to what came before.

Lotus had been with the larger dog, Bones, when she disappeared. Tenants on the first floor heard him early one morning scratching at the door that led to Lotus' basement apartment. Lotus' other dog, the little female, scratched from inside the apartment where she had been closed in with a bathtub full of water and a pail full of dry dog food.

She heard all this indirectly. She had, at the time, been preoccupied with Charles Danson. They stayed late, working on the paper mill case. "Sue them for defamation, conspiracy and interference with business," she said of the protestors.

"You're good. You're very good," Charles Danson said, grinning.

There was no funeral, only phone calls from their mother, crying about her husband's refusal to discuss a memorial service. The tears soon turned to bickering.

She went to Charles Danson, asked him what to do, legally, to declare her sister dead and finish it once and for all.

"Check the Marriage Act," he had said.

"But she's not married."

"Does she own property? Any insurance policies?"

"No."

"Then, legally speaking, she doesn't exist."

Janice trips over a boulder, sees a post marked 6. RELIC OF THE ICE AGE. She's been crying for the last half kilo-metre, going through the bush away from the river. Lotus was so light, maybe she believed she could walk on the surface of the river, reach the other side and keep on going. Maybe she succeeded, moving on ahead of Janice once again. This last marker identifies the remains of the ice sheet that covered this region and the *erratics*, boulders that were trapped in the ice and transported here by a glacier.

She saw Bones much later, a subdued brown rag in the corner of her parents' kitchen, but she knows his frighten-ing shape from all her dreams: fur spiked with ice like a porcupine, icicles dripping from his blue collar and the tips of his ears, a hoary frost around his mouth. Janice has looked into his brown eyes, held his big head in her hands just the way Lotus held the head of her favourite dog, the one she left behind the night she disappeared, and waited for some message to cross over. She saw her reflection in the dog's eyes, oddly skewed, eyes startled and wide, not at all the way she thinks she appears to the rest of the world.

CLAIMING THE BODY

My mother has refused to claim and bury her brother's body. All week, the image of him wrapped in sheets has threatened to unravel in my mind.

I was informed of my uncle's death as an afterthought to an aimless conversation with my father. I am sure he is drinking, although he claims to be sober now. He often calls me in the morning and offers to bring me groceries. He was trying to talk me into a crate of cantaloupes.

"You can store them here in the basement fridge," he insisted. "I can bring one over anytime." When I declined, he moved on. "Well, come out for a barbecue."

"It's winter."

"So what?" A challenge in this, a not-so-kind tone.

"Oh, by the way, your Uncle Donald died," he added. "The hospital keeps calling your mother." He laughed. I could see him leaning his huge belly on the doorframe into the dining room where he stands when he's talking on the phone.

"They think she's supposed to deal with it," he said. "He put her down as his next of kin."

"When's the funeral?"

"She's not his next of kin. It's up to Simon."

His obtuseness has always amazed me. My cousin Simon's strangeness eventually crossed the line into schizophrenia and he has been institutionalized since my Aunt Helen's death. He is older than me, always pale, his speech so soft you might think it is an echo. He watches his hands as though they have a life of their own. Hard to imagine him capable of anything, except that strange vigil. And by some quirk of family wisdom, he was named my godfather, to "give him some responsibility," when his illness was in its early stages. I was supposed to save him, and I do look like a substantial weight in his arms in family photos, my white christening gown hanging down to his knees. He's staring off into space.

Everything he gave me was white, to match the costumes I wore for each sacrament. I still have the white rosary, a white satin scapula of St. Christopher that I pinned to my undershirt under the white cloak for confirmation. For my first communion, he gave me a tiny prayer book that slipped into a hard pearly pocket. The pages were almost transparent, rimmed with gold, the letters so small I could barely read them. I couldn't see him as he stood beside me for photographs because the veil obscured my peripheral vision. Now I know that his mother, my Aunt Helen, must have chosen these presents, so perfect was their girlish virtue.

"Simon's the next of kin," my father repeated.

"That's splitting hairs," I said, shivering at the term.

I recall, in vivid detail, the clothes my mother wore when I was young. Particularly, a white fitted dress gathered in just below her breasts by a shocking line of blood-red roses appliquéd to her rib cage. The dress was lined with slippery silk, cool against my face when I hid in her closet.

Next to it was my mother's wedding dress, wrapped in plastic. Pearl buttons, a satin bodice and pinned to it, a little Juliet cap with veil. For years, that dress was too large. I didn't need to remove the plastic to know it would never fit, that the bodice would be unpleasantly airy, the dress leaning sideways off my childish frame like an abandoned house about to collapse. And by the time it fit, my body an echo of hers, I was already gone, her closet and her secrets irrelevant to me. Until now.

"She could hide any flaw," my mother said of her sister-in-law's sewing. For that reason or some other, Aunt Helen and my uncle had been taken along on my parents' honeymoon. Beside the wedding dress hung a scarlet satin cocktail dress with spaghetti straps and a black-and-peach dress with sequined flowers sewn onto the bodice. These were from her trousseau, or later, from her days as a wife in the officers' mess, before my father's drinking made outings in such elegant clothes a travesty. Then, she put away the heels with the pointed toes and put on the flat loafers she always wears in the house, her feet clicking up and down the hard-wood floor. She bought a bland succession of earth-toned jackets she wears indoors, even in summer.

My mother has never asked me to make clothes for her, even though clothes are my livelihood now. I work out of an office in the basement. What would I recommend, if she did? The pastel, unrevealing clothes of the elderly, so often contradicted by the vivid red slash of lipstick many older women favour, a reminder of their youth? The mourning clothes of old European cultures, sadness worn on the sleeve?

"What do you think, Hazel?" Since Luke left, I find myself talking to my dressmaker's dummy, standing before her blank, hard torso, imagining the right cut, the right cloth for a client. She is headless, footless, just a swell of womanly shape. I named her Hazel after the hurricane that accompanied my birth, the only part of my own birth story I know. First the low pressure brought on a migraine, then the pains. My mother stepped out of the car at the hospital into a puddle, ankle-deep.

Hazel's breasts will never sag, but there are no nipples, nothing that isn't functional. She expands or contracts to suit the client and her heart is encased in hard, pink plastic. I ease the pins from my mouth and slide my hand along her smooth, cool bosom. She's worn the clothes of a hundred women: women with events to attend, men to excite and please, needs to conceal; women with a private pain that seems to come flooding out when I touch one spot or another.

I'm good at my job. I listen sympathetically and still keep enough professional distance to reach under a breast to pin a dart, place my thumb against a warm groin as I measure for length. Women seem to feel a need to explain their bodies to me, the scars, the stretch marks, the places their flesh has swelled beyond their wills.

"Did you know that at thirty-seven a woman's eggs start to die?" one of my customers tells me. All day I walk around feeling transparent and mysteriously bereft.

This morning my father calls again, but now my uncle's body seems to have replaced grocery shopping as the main topic. He tells me the hospital called two more times. They don't refer to it as "making arrangements" anymore. They talk about claiming the body.

"So, is she making the arrangements?" I ask, retreating to a word that still offers a shred of decency.

"I don't know how they got her name," he answers. "Donald must have written it down somewhere."

"What did he die of?"

"Oh, nothing, really. He was just an old drunk," my father says.

"Dad, I have to go now. I've got work to do."

"When are you coming to see your mother?" he asks accusatively. He must be drinking. That is the only time his emotions are this transparent. He is really asking this for himself. When I visit my mother, she seems only mildly interested in me. We sit side by side on the couch for brief, pleasant conversations. But my father is attentive in an anxious way. In his old age, he's been taken over by grand gestures, constant shopping excursions, loading my fridge with produce that wilts before I even remember it's there.

"You wouldn't believe what fertility treatments do to your sex life," she says, stepping up on the platform. Each customer has a colour, a texture, rather than a name. This woman bristles, is sharp, like a crinoline, and she is a hungry colour, like orange. It seems discordant that the dress I am making for her is cool, silky blue. But she insists I call her by name: Julia, a name conjuring up easy, naive fertility.

"Graphing your every intimacy, noting details like position, how long I stayed in bed afterwards." This is a very intimate thing to be telling me, but I look up and see her looking off into space.

"How short to do you want this to be?" I ask her, brushing the light blue fabric against her strong calves. She says she's bloated from the fertility treatments, but her flesh is firm and girlish and I realize how few of the bodies I touch in a week haven't had children.

"Long and I want room in case I grow."

I see her fingers crossed behind her back. I know her body well after several fittings. My services were a gift from her female relatives, a pick-me-up antishower after the last pregnancy failed. She is tired around the eyes, and strained. Her body is lithe and almost quivering with tension, impossible that its vitality hasn't burst into new life.

"But the worst was when we had to run into the clinic

right after sex to check if something was killing off his sperm. He's got to be in the mood no matter what. I never thought pornography could be my friend."

I stop a minute.

"What?" she asks, looking down at me.

"I was just remembering something," I tell her, turning my attention again to the hem.

"What? I've been standing here for two weeks telling *you* my sex life ... "

"I just realized when my marriage started to go downhill. His vasectomy. It never really occurred to me, until now."

As I expected, she does not ask for more details. She glances down at me, stricken, and a little angry, too. That's good, I think. It's only through anger that she'll let go.

I'm a little shaken, too, by this unwelcome sense of his physical being somewhere out there beyond me. Suddenly so real again: the colour of the skin on the inside of his wrists, what the pulse felt like on my tongue, the length of his thigh beside me in the car, all the vulnerable physical details that punctuate a marriage, the thousand small inti-macies that weave you together.

"Hazel, you'd be a big disappointment to a man. Just imagine his face when he slips into you. Dead air. " I laugh, sounding demented, I know, which is why my children only come home once they know I'm out of the basement.

"But even you could be full of surprises, couldn't you?" I tell her, remembering something that happened to a girl in one of my art classes in university. She was a blade-thin girl who lived in the same house as my friend Sue. We thought this girl was pretentious, urban-bohemian, with a brush cut years before it came into style. She found an old mannequin in an alley behind a row of shops, obviously from the Fifties. The body was more lush than any mannequin that's been in store windows since 1968, with a little belly sticking out, a smooth airless slope between her legs, red hair matted and smelling mouldy, as though it had been stored in a root cellar. The mannequin stood in the living room, heated up by spring sun. My friend hated it, couldn't stand the smell of it, but everyone who lived in the house voted and the mannequin stayed. Until the day a nest of spiders burst out of her head. Exploded. Thousands of baby spiders scattering to every corner of the house. After months of stamping and screaming whenever anyone took a cup out of the cupboard, everyone moved out.

"I'm going to ask my sister to be an egg donor. I'll try anything at this point," Julia says above me. Her slim hips are under my hands. I'm checking that I've compensated, as one of her hips is slightly higher than the other. This is the last visit. The dress is nearly done.

"It used to be that women were stuck. But it's changing every day. After our three attempts failed, we were advised to go to counselling, try to work it through, and to *get on with our lives*. Don't you hate it when they say that, as though life is a consolation prize?"

My mother used that exact phrase after Luke left. She was watering her ferns in the blinding afternoon sun, not looking at me.

"Go on with your life. So, you're disappointed. You'll get over it," she said. Then she walked away to the kitchen, clicking in her sensible shoes.

I move around her, stooping to check the levelness of the hem, but she continues talking, picking up speed. She tells me eggs may one day be taken, like corneas, from accident victims, or harvested from the ovaries of aborted fetuses. She tells me this is the miracle of our age, just as the throwing aside of crutches was a miracle of the past. I wonder what it would be like to discover you're the child of a mother who never lived. I think about a young woman who walks away from an abortion clinic, relieved and sad, only to become a grandmother before she has even become a mother. We have enough of our ghosts to put to rest without having them rise up before us in physical form.

When I was about thirteen, I searched every crevice of my mother's life with a furtive excitement. I searched through her drawers tangled with old girdles, unearthed strange female equipment in a quilted metallic bag, noticed the monthly cycle of her used sanitary pads in the wastebasket in the bathroom, still humming with her heat. I couldn't say what I was looking for. Was it revenge that made me cut up the cocktail dresses and velvet skirts stored in plastic in the back of her closet? I was just making costumes; she had seemed only mildly interested in the results. I scissored in half the white dress with the appliquéd roses and pressed the roses themselves in a book of fairy tales I kept under my bed. Around that time, I asked her to tell me about my birth. She told me about the hurricane, but skipped right over the birth itself.

"But what was it like in the hospital?" I pressed; what I wanted to know I couldn't ask, so this would have to do. She eyed me with something that might have been hostility. She told me she had delivered my oldest brother nine months after her wedding, my sister twelve months after that and me the very next year.

"I wasn't really conscious," she said. "You do all the work, that's why they call it labour, but then they put you to sleep."

When my own daughter was born, I was so sure she was wrong. The sheer energy of pushing her into the world lived on in a torrid, violent mother love for a year or two after each of my children.

Then it changes, imperceptibly. It was like the veils Renaissance painters used to hang in their studios so they could paint objects as if from a great distance. Now it's as if something is pulled across my daughter's face so that it seems I haven't seen her in days, even though we live together. Yet she takes my scarves, my gloves. I find my hairbrush on her bed, my earrings, bright lures dropped on her bedroom floor. I confront her angrily with the evidence. She smiles like the Mona Lisa, as if this reaction is exactly what she needs.

"What do they do to unclaimed bodies in morgues?" I ask the svelte woman stepping up onto my small, round platform. She is an internist at the local hospital and this is the third evening gown I've made for her. This one is dramatic, a blood-red velvet tapered and flaring out from her thin hips, making her look almost voluptuous. She intends to wear the dress to the National Arts Centre, where her nephew will be performing for the first time.

"Are you trying to plan the perfect crime?" she asks me, playfully.

"No, I'm trying to prevent one. My uncle's body is in the morgue and nobody can agree whose responsibility it is to claim it."

She looks down at me, considering carefully.

"You may not like the answer," she says.

"Maybe not. But I'd rather know."

"Medical science, for research or teaching," she tells me. "Sometimes private industry makes an arrangement."

"For what?"

"For experiments," she says, raising her arms to check the lift of the skirt. "Look, I don't like telling you this."

"What kind of experiments?"

"Car manufacturers, for testing."

She has avoided that vaguely comical term, "crash test dummies," and I don't know whether to laugh or cry. I fill my mouth with pins, turn away.

When my father calls again, he doesn't mention my uncle's body. It's been a few days. Something must have happened, but if there had been a ceremony, I would have heard.

"There's a sale on steaks at the IGA," he says.

"We're vegetarian. You know that."

"It's not good for those kids."

"Better than booze!" I say. He's silent for a minute. Then he moves on as though I haven't said a thing.

"Your mother's had quite a week," he says. A conspiratorial tone.

"You mean Uncle Donald's death?"

"They called her over and over. She told them he had a son."

"So, what happened?"

"They must have found Simon. They said a public funeral was arranged."

I can't imagine my cousin, Simon, arranging anything. "Public funeral" sounds like a euphemism. It probably means his body is now in the public domain. My uncle's aging, unwanted body, to be taken apart in the hands of strangers or sent into mock oblivion over and over in cars crashed against concrete walls. My mother's brother to live out other people's tragedies, other people's accidents. I barely knew him. I remember his voice and my father's, late on summer nights as they sat drinking in the backyard, their gaiety one notch too loud, drifting in my open window when I was trying to sleep. Once when they were visiting, my Aunt Helen, who died of a brain tumour when I was twelve, gave me a tiny pair of folding binoculars.

"To look into the future," she told me, slipping the little gold chain over my head.

I peered through them backward and saw my mother, too small, far away down a long tunnel, laughing as Aunt

Helen put her arm around her. She was always able to make my mother laugh.

"I want to talk to her," I tell him.

He says nothing.

"I want to talk to her. Where is she?"

"It's cold out today," he says.

"I'm asking you a straight question." But he's already gone.

HOMEWRECKER

He started with bars on the basement windows. A natural concern, at his stage of life, to want the house secure. Even though they were both home much of the time now that he was retired from the university, she thought the bars were a good idea. The tree-lined street where they lived, in an expensive older neighbourhood full of young professionals, was empty during the day. Just a few weeks before, their neighbour's alarm system had sounded and she'd watched through the sheers as the police car sped to the curb.

Daniel had been her professor when they met, with a wife and child. They were once fearless, but now she felt she was getting old along with him. The world belonged to others who coveted and lied, who burst in and took what they wanted.

So he bought two-foot lengths of iron bars, drilled holes in the window frames and, with much grunting, pushed them horizontal, snug against the filmy glass. Daniel called her downstairs to see what he had done. Stephanie descended the wooden steps ahead of him, fearing slightly that he would topple onto her from behind. He had gained a great deal of weight over the last ten years and he frequently lost his balance.

The basement was where he went to drink. He often surfaced from the half-finished room with a cut on his chin, or above the eye, as though he had been involved in a bar fight down there. A buddy from AA had been helping him finish it, had done the wiring, but he mysteriously disappeared from Daniel's life before the lights were secured into the ceiling. They hung by coloured wires, were probably responsible for some of the cuts, but she had created another version of the story. To her family, who had never approved of the marriage, she would give a breezy account: "Daniel's hacked himself up again doing renovations. I tell him, let's just hire someone, but he's so stubborn." To his daughter, who stopped by with his grandchildren once a week, she had become, over the years, more pointed, almost accusatory, "Look what he's done to his face. This has got to stop." Stephanie didn't know why she bothered telling Nicole anything. She certainly didn't offer any solace. Nicole would narrow those golden eyes of hers and say something vaguely hostile. "Has anything changed? Haven't you gotten used to it by now?"

Today was Tuesday, so she could walk through the basement without fear. He never drank on Tuesdays. He went to his AA meetings sober, stood up with the rest of them and said, "Hello. My name is Daniel and I'm an alcoholic." She had gone last winter to his first birthday of sobriety, sat on a wooden chair in a church basement alongside Nicole, the grandchildren, Dexter and Drew, and surprisingly, his first wife, Marie.

Marie had cried throughout his speech and his eyes, too, had filled with tears as he admitted to a room full of strangers what a bad husband he had been, a terrible father, always working, always late for supper, caught up in psychological arguments in smoky student pubs. "Rats running through mazes," he always called behaviourism with a dismissive wave of his hand. She knew. She had been there, in those smoky pubs, entranced by his passion for Freud and Jung, who were unfashionable by then. She remembered a phrase she loved: "the family romance." He said it in crowded classrooms and bars with a raised eyebrow, his seductive, confidential tone singling out each listener, promising intrigues, delights and betrayals worthy of any royal court. She had wanted to pass through those shadowy doorways, gain entry to the inner sanctum. She thought her life would keep unfolding, revealing new chambers she could explore until she finally reached some place of still, absolute clarity.

But instead, she had found herself in a church basement full of people who smoked the air into a blue haze and fidgeted with their stained hands. She focused on her own breathing, imagining the stains the smoke was leaving on her lungs, angry that she had to sit there and hear him reduce those exhilarating times to drunkenness. She had been offended by his ex-wife's hand squeezing her forearm, drawing her back to listen as he talked about his need for her support. She hated to hear that sanctimonious tone in his voice, "my wife, Stephanie ..." Marie touching her, finally acknowledging her after all these years, now that he had repudiated everything that had brought them together.

Usually, when she and Daniel were in public together, they remained attentive to the old story. Other women her age would ask her where she had met Daniel, noticing that he was of a different generation. She would mention the electricity that had passed between them when he lectured, telling them he was once her professor. "How romantic," they would say and she would smile gratefully. She looked over briefly at Marie and a touch of that old arrogance returned. She saw a woman past her prime, a woman who cried in public.

Stephanie had listened, angry and unmoved, to the other testimonials. A man who was celebrating his eighteenth year of sobriety, and a woman, miraculously *born again* and twenty-three years off the bottle. Could they be trusted? As the night wore on, the tinny falseness of the stories grew brighter. Perhaps it was bragging, she thought, all these anecdotes, outrageous pasts. A man who hung his son out a tenth-storey window, holding him by the ankles. A woman who stashed booze in a full diaper pail, so drunk most of the time she forgot to twist the top tightly closed. Try as she might to be empathetic, Stephanie couldn't fathom drinking gin tinged blue with Diaper Pure. After the meeting, they drove home in silence.

He was now working toward his second-year medal from AA, although he'd started drinking in secret again after his big first birthday celebration. Not right away, she didn't think, but somewhere in the long darkness of January and February he had descended to his basement again.

"No one will get in here," he told her, pointing at the bars.

"Oh, Daniel. Look what you did to the frame. You've gouged holes in it."

He talked on, pleased with his work. "Look. Three-quarter inch bars. Can't budge that," he said, reaching up and grasping with his big hands.

Since he'd stopped teaching, his hands seemed to have changed. They were puffier, larger, like the hands of the men in his family who had spent their working lives framing houses, hauling bags of feed from warehouses, who drank hard, swore hard, raised smudged beer glasses with hands calloused and cut. His retirement had returned him to his origins, despite all his plans.

He had told her they would travel and that he would write that book on Freud he'd never had time for. The retirement had been arranged by the university a few years earlier than he had wanted. Although he never told her why, she had assumed there had been complaints. Near the end, he was rarely sober, even when he went to work. "Pressure," he called it, but retirement didn't take any stress from him. It seemed to have discouraged him and once he no longer had anywhere to go in the mornings, he withdrew into the basement and ceased to mention Vienna, or the tall Victorian house in London that Anna Freud had preserved after her father's death.

Not long after he secured the basement, she heard the sound of glass shattering. She sat playing Chopin on the piano he had bought for her early in their relationship. She had quit school even before they married, unsettled by the voyeurism focused now on her. These voyeurs were the same young women in her classes who had once reported his every move to her, pressured her up onto the darkened stage in the basement café of the university centre to play the piano, saying, "Go on. Do it before he leaves for his two o'clock class." And she had, her fingers trembling as they slipped over the familiar runs of Chopin. It was a victory for all of them that he sat in his corner listening well past two o'clock. Eventually, though, she opted to step down, into the home he bought for her.

Back then, she played the piano every day; her crescendos were their crescendos. She favoured music full of weather: rainstorms, brooding thunderheads, the passionate play of light dazzling, as he dazzled her, kissing her neck as he tiptoed behind her, raising the hair on the back of her neck. She was sheltered by this tall, narrow house in an older neighbourhood, setting their lives apart from the suburbs where Marie and Nicole remained.

She hadn't known much about his life before, had preferred not to ask too many questions. It was surprising how little she knew even now. He told her nothing. It was Nicole who provided details. That was how she learned that Marie was not, in fact, a suburban housewife, but a piano teacher. Stephanie had been playing Mendelssohn's "Song Without Words" when Nicole, about sixteen and with them on most weekends as part of the custody arrangement, had said loudly from the door, "Oh, God, you play that so *cha cha*, just like Mom's students. I have to hear kids do that every day at home. Give it a rest, huh?" And then she was gone, her voice lilting down the basement stairs, calling for her father to play a game of ping-pong. Stephanie had held her tongue at the time, but she felt uneasy.

Stephanie's mother had pushed her on, graduating one grade, then the next, saying, "It's something a woman can do at home. And you'll always be popular at parties." But parties had seemed irrelevant during that first year of sneaking around with Daniel, so she had let her technique slip just when it mattered most. She played for atmosphere, instead. She played so she could relive, over and over again, their coming together, and no one would know, not even Daniel. When they were finally living together, she played only for herself. She waited for her life with Daniel to really begin and in the meantime tutored and typed graduate theses, volunteered in small rooms, pointing at brightly coloured drawings and tapping out rhythms. The children didn't speak to her, barely seemed to notice her, humming and rocking themselves into trances.

Stephanie's repertoire on the piano diminished to the few pieces she could get right. Mostly nocturnes. Often she would stop mid measure and stare at the notes before her, or get up from the piano with a chord unresolved. One of her teachers had said that was the sign of a poor musician, but what did it matter now?

She lifted her hands suddenly when she heard the shattering glass. Someone breaking in! Another, less unpleasant, possibility surfaced. Not a thought, exactly, but a scenario that did not cause her dread or panic, as she would have expected. His weight falling against a window. She imagined sweeping the glass from his face, then placing her mouth on his, breathing, listening, breathing, her lip cut by the shards. She would try, but it would be too late.

Cautiously she opened the door that led into the garage and whispered, "Daniel? Are you all right?"

"Jesus, Mary and Joseph!" he swore. "Looka that." He was standing in the garage doorway to the backyard. She turned on the light and saw him swinging the door on its hinges with a hammer in his hand, shards of glass on the cement floor reflecting light.

"What on earth have you done?"

"Just boarding up this window and —"

"Boarding up the window," she interrupted. "And making this look like a slum. Why?" She couldn't keep the irritation out of her voice.

"Electric doors on the garage, bars, dead bolts and then this back door with nothing but glass. Does that make sense? I was nailing a board over it and crash, a nail went through the goddamn glass."

"You're depreciating the value of this house!"

"So what?" he said, suddenly angry, swaying on his feet as he looked at her menacingly. "Who do you think will live to take full advantage anyway?"

She was about to slam the door when Nicole's voice sounded behind her.

"Hi. The kids are in the backyard," she warned them as she came up closer, close enough for Stephanie to hear her quick breathing.

"Hi, Dad. We were just on the way to the pool. Such a hot day. Dexter and Drew were impossible. Sometimes I can't take it, being locked in the house all day. Do you want a cup of tea?" she called over Stephanie's shoulder.

"Sure, sweetie. Tell the kids to stay clear." It amazed Stephanie how Daniel was able to come out with sober sentences when anybody else was around.

"What are you doing there, Dad? Home improvements?" Nicole teased him. "You never were much around the house. Mom was ready to kill you when you started to dig up the backyard for the pool, shovelful by shovelful."

"Well, I'm alive to tell the tale, aren't I?"

"Only because you didn't have to face the music!" Nicole laughed.

"Well, it's a wonder your mother didn't have my head on a stake. You know how she loves her roses."

Stephanie didn't wait for the next phase of this conversation. She had been witness to one exactly like it many times before. The content might change, but it was always the same. Nicole pulling him back, Daniel willing to follow, at least in his imagination.

"He's either smashed or smashing things up. Sometimes both," she said to Nicole as she walked away. "Keep the kids away from him. All we need is bleeding feet."

She hadn't intended her words to sound so cold. She liked the twins, even though she had never had children of her own. He hadn't wanted to be caught in the "same old maze." Drew and Dexter, though, were unexpected delights: two blond heads bobbing somewhere around her thickening waist, their bright faces beaming up at hers like searchlights. Secretly, she had hoped they would find some name for her, to recognize her place in the family, but

Nicole had instructed them when they were just two or three, "That's Stephanie. Grandpa's wife. Too hard to say? OK, how about Steph. Call her Steph." She had drawled the sound for them, with a flat "e." She had heard the distaste in Nicole's voice, her name pronounced "staph," like the infection. Nicole said her name, when she said it all, with about as much enthusiasm. Nicole never left the children here alone.

She was too agitated to do anything but hover in the kitchen, hearing Drew and Dexter argue over who was to hold the dustpan, who the broom, as Nicole and Daniel swept the glass away, splintering sounds punctuated by their laughter. She left the kitchen to them, placing a tea cozy over the forgotten tea, and went upstairs to lie in the dim blue room she'd once shared with Daniel.

She knew what would happen next. She would continue, for a time, to hear Nicole's voice, good-humoured and slightly too loud, and Daniel's voice, a low grumble. The children's voices would fade into the silence of Nicole's car. Then there would be heavy footsteps, growing more faint as Daniel descended into the basement, followed by a suffocating hush. Only when he had retreated would she rise and slip into the TV room. The two of them would scuttle all night from room to room. She would catch sight of his back disappearing around a corner. Perhaps he caught a glimpse of her sandaled foot from his vantage point in the hall, but they avoided each other. Always on the move, always shrinking back. Sometimes she wondered if he stood silently behind doors, around corners when she drew too close. He seemed to permeate the house so that she was never quite sure where he was. Sometimes he would spend the night in the basement or surface and sleep in odd places, scaring her when she rose in the mornings to see a wild dark shape curled up on the living room floor.

She could not predict what he would do to the house next, even though a pattern seemed to be emerging. The crash of recycling boxes early in the morning, the metal drag of a ladder being moved, made her sit up suddenly in her bed, alert and panicky.

She didn't have to wait long. A thud seemed to shake the floor beneath her bed. She thought it was an earthquake. Stand in a doorway, she told herself. The house might fall, but the doorway would still stand after everything else was in rubble. In a moment, though, her mind cleared, and she remembered that it was late summer and Daniel was rising early, his anxious pattern before autumn brought him down into a sedentary depression.

When she saw what he had done, she knew he must have spent all night in the basement, surfacing just for this. He was kneeling before the bright, open space that had once been their front door. The light was confusing. Ridiculously, she thought of a man kneeling, facing Mecca, in the throes of a revelation, but then she heard him gasp and grunt with effort, caught a whiff of sweet half-rotted rye, before she saw the chisel and hammer in his hand.

"Daniel!"

"Just gimme a hand here, will you?" he said, indicating the corner of the door lying flat on the floor of the front hallway.

"Daniel, why?" she asked, feeling tears prickle in her eyes. It was one of her hidden vices; she was what her mother would have called house-proud. Her crystal glasses lined up under the dim light in the china cabinet, the sheers, fine as veils, the bevelled moulding around the ceiling, gave her airy, wordless pleasure, the only kind of pleasure she trusted anymore.

"Why are you destroying the house?"

"Just fixing things. The damn thing got stuck," he answered, bending again, smashing the chisel with the hammer and sending a long chip of wood flying.

"What got stuck? Nothing's wrong with the front door," she said, trying to be calm.

"Dead bolt won't work."

"But you've destroyed the whole door," she said, and looking further, "and the frame!"

He stopped, leaned back unsteadily.

"Dead bolt was wrecked, finished. Damn doorknob won't turn, so I took off the door by the hinges." He shook his head sadly. "The sucker wouldn't come, so ..." He raised the chisel as if toasting her. "I fixed it! Well, almost."

"Why don't you stop right now?"

He was suddenly angry. "Stop what?"

"Stop all of it. Stop *fixing* things. Just stop it. You're no good at it."

"Mind your own business." He turned and started working again, grunting with the exertion of lifting the door off the floor, placing it into the gouged opening. It would not fit and he teetered unsteadily before lowering it again.

She turned away helplessly, reached the phone and called Nicole.

"Nicole," she said bluntly. "He's at it again. Could you come over and talk some sense into him?"

"At what again?" Nicole answered obliquely. Stephanie was sure she did this on purpose.

"He's taken a hammer and chisel to the front door ..."

There was silence on the other end for a moment. Then Nicole's voice saying, "That's between you and him."

Still, she wasn't surprised when she heard Nicole's car before it rounded the corner. Stephanie was relieved to see that she was alone. She walked up the driveway, stopped suddenly when she saw the place where the front door was supposed to be.

"Dad?" she called. "Where's the front door? Dad?"

Daniel stopped his haphazard chiselling of the door held between his knees long enough to lose his balance. The door slipped and smashed its stained glass window against the banister, raining blue and green shards all over the pale carpet. It had once been fluid, mermaids swirling in icy blues. Then Nicole was on her hands and knees, gathering fragments of the glass in cupped hands.

"My stained glass. You broke my stained glass," she said, softly, incredulously.

"Sweetie, don't cut your hands," Daniel said.

Nicole looked up at him, her voice tense. "I don't care. I made that for you. I could never make anything like it again. How could you?" She swept with her hands, red arcs of her blood streaking the pale carpet at the foot of the stairs.

"Nicole, stop that right now. You'll hurt yourself," Daniel's baritone suddenly sounded perfectly sober. Stephanie heard that familiar timbre in his voice, the man she once loved who saw everything clearly, the man who would speak forbidden truths while she sat dreamily in his class all those years ago.

"I'm not a child. In case you hadn't noticed, I grew up. You weren't there for it."

Nicole straightened her back, sat back on her heels, letting both of them see her face livid with tears.

"This is just like the pool, isn't it?" she said. "That summer before you left. All mapped out with stakes and string. Those scrappy pieces of paper you jotted estimates on. All lies. And that hole. You left Mom to fill it. You always leave everyone to clean up your messes. Why should we stop now?"

The pool story was one of their favourites. Stephanie had heard it many times before, but never had she heard the dark counterpoint beneath the words.

Stephanie inched back and sat on the stairs, letting them act out what was left of their family romance. She looked beyond them to the gaping wound where the front door should have been, a way in or a way out.

"Nicole," he was saying softly, sinking into his wrinkled clothes, "a lot was going on then."

"I'll bet," Nicole said.

TWENTY-TWO NIGHTS

W hen they speak of the drugs, their voices are soft and melancholy, like the low voices of women in restaurants bent together over a candle confiding about a man. *Valium. Lorazepam. Ativan.* These words with decorous classical rhythms, like the names of knights, recur during the weekly evenings when they meet in each other's homes. They confess what it felt like the first night, the first week, the first month of lying down, miraculously, without that feeling of being alone. The slow, warm dissolve of fear and tension, their skulls softening. This was the same for all for them. Repetitive thoughts gave way to a foamy, floating feeling that made the world seem benevolent, the bed welcoming, their own thoughts positive and turned forward to a near future that included sleep. They knew it couldn't last. Larger and larger doses. Poisoned kidneys, the shakes, crying fits. Poisoned hearts.

When they aren't talking about drugs, they talk about men. Tonight they are spurred on by Carla's grandfather's dire warning: *Even one spot of blood on your skirt and he's not responsible,* men as sharks, sniffing blood from across the room. The other women join in with their own stories, some in sudden bursts of tears, some offhand. Slow, predatory seductions, violent ruptures of clothes and flesh; Anna hears them all.

She starts to say, "I was followed once, when I was young. For almost two years." When they all turn their attention to her, she stops. Nothing happened. The story has no ending. She only remembers the man's indifferent stare and the way her heart pounded whenever she saw a white car parked at a curb. She remembers her fear, but also her anger. The bath was the only place she was allowed to be alone, sinking beneath the surface, water deafening her, dulling sounds outside the closed door. Or in sleep between unsettled dreams. These were the only times she felt truly herself. Anna knows this isn't much to offer. Fear of possibility instead of reality. Yet all her life, since he inexplicably disappeared, she has felt a glass wall around her. Beyond that, she sees the sharks circling, feels the slow seep of blood out of her body, and rises to leave.

The women in the group thank tonight's hostess, then move toward the line of parallel elevators. Anna slips ahead of them in the hollow-sounding hallway. She is ready after an evening of intimacy to lose herself in her own company.

"Good night," she says over her shoulder, too softly for them to hear because she has her head down, focusing on the orange geometric design of the carpeting, the hushed synthetic scrape of her shoes, the elevator signal that lights up like a halo. Doors slide open, metallic grey as sea flesh, so easy, and she's relieved to step inside, alone, tripping over the lip, lunging headfirst toward the floor before balancing again.

She's tired. Weeks without sleep, it seems. Twenty-two nights, to be exact, without shelter, without pills. But instead of making the world more dreamy, this sleeplessness heightens her senses. Light swarms on the metal wall. The rumble of the elevator starting down is not something she hears, but feels in the pit of her stomach, the way she used to feel fireworks when they exploded above her, the way sound under water is not sound, but a wave of power that can kill prey.

The elevator slips through space so smoothly, she feels the suspended attention that makes enclosed spaces bearable, then a strange bouncing as it stops at the twenty-first floor. A man steps through the open doors, tripping over the lip. A soft curse, "oh fuck," then he turns, nonchalantly poking his thumb in the depression marked B. The doors slide shut, then silence and stillness. He leans over, unhooking his hand from his leather belt and jabs the B just below the lit G again. A little lurch, then nothing. She stands behind him, transfixed by his presence, his breathing, his tanned shoulders swelling out of his sleeveless T-shirt, his dusty jeans. A sudden drop and her stomach jerks. She feels a lifting in her head, inside her left ear, and looks down at his steel-toed boots to orient herself, gulps a little dry air. This man is all steel and muscle, even the hair curling on the back of his neck is metallic bronze.

They free-fall for a second, then bounce as though they're on the end of an elastic band. The elevator quivers between floors, stops. She feels something rise in her throat. Her first thought is of the blood leaking from her. What will she do if she's stuck in here so long that the pad needs to be changed? She has one in her purse, but how will she do it?

They stand without acknowledging each other and wait for something to happen. Finally he acknowledges her, saying, "Try nineteen." She does, eagerly. The elevator shudders, drops in that free-floating feeling and bounces again to a stop between the eighteenth and nineteenth floors.

"It didn't stop at nineteen," Anna says, relieved to hear her voice sound matter-of-fact.

"Try hitting eighteen," he tells her, a little louder this time. She does. A soft rumble, a series of slipping jerks and they free-fall to the seventeenth floor.

"Shit," he says, kicking the door slightly with his steel-toed boot. "We're stuck."

Hearing it said out loud makes her even more light-headed. She believes that if only she could lie down, she would fall asleep right now. So familiar to her, this feeling, as though she has been trapped in this elevator for twenty-two nights. The same feeling she has in her bed, lying flat, as though there is somewhere else she is supposed to be. If she could only find that place, she would fall asleep and leave behind the terrible vigilance that keeps her turning through the night. Instead of up and down, the elevator feels like it's moving in circles, like the rides she remembers from her childhood. Teacups and saucers spinning around on a flat surface. "The Scrambler" that her parents inno-cently suggested, not realizing what was in store. Wrenched back and forth and round in circles at the same time. Even if the sun-darkened men taking tickets, flipping safety catches, crouching to check connections, could hear you cry out, they'd only smirk at each other, bored.

"Can it fall all the way?" Anna asks.

"There's probably a brake," he says before they feel a sudden rush, fall what feels like two floors.

That shuddering bounce stops them again. Then silence. They don't speak, don't acknowledge each other. She stares ahead and realizes after a few moments that she is staring directly at a red lipstick mark, puckered lips, on the sliding metal doors just near the slit. Every line of the lips is lit up. The kiss is saucy and slightly open. She hopes he doesn't notice it, too, or notice her noticing it. She's suddenly afraid of him. She hears her heart beating in her left ear. She tries to breathe through her nose so that he won't hear her. He's heard her voice, trusting, and looking to him for reassurance. The kiss mark almost glistens, scarlet and fresh. Her own lips tingle cold, metal on skin. A small round mirror is mounted in the back corner above their heads. Mounted so women can see, before getting on, if someone is hiding, squeezed against the control panel. When she glances up at the mirror, she's suddenly shocked by the sight of the back of his head, harsh and unnaturally large, and the red kiss mark swimming off near his left shoulder like a tropical fish. She can't see anything of herself.

He reaches out and presses all the buttons, up and down. Suddenly, twenty-eight lights are burning a calm, steady yellow. She reaches out and jabs at the red emergency button. It is the first time in her life she has ever done anything like this and if she were alone, she would probably settle down and wait. EMERGENCY written in white on bright red, but they can't hear a thing. She expected something dramatic. She doesn't expect this complete nothing. Her legs are shaking under her long cotton skirt. She wants to sit on the floor and pretend they can wait, bored and calm, for release.

She tries not to think of the long reckless fall, the crash as they hit bottom. Longing for the soft, slow descent through that cool shaft that narrows and then enlarges into unconsciousness. Making it to the bottom without that jerk of fear that some doctors have told her is an electrical discharge in her brain, other doctors have called a fear of death, fear of men, fear of loss of control, and on and on, with no solution but the little pills with the elegant names. For years she sank down the shaft encased in a strong protective shell of sleepiness without dreams. Her nights in shining armour. Impervious and completely untouchable. Sleep so otherworldly she might as well have been lying, composed, under glass for a hundred years.

He moves forward, nose to the doors, mouth near the red lipstick mark he doesn't seem to notice, and squeezes his fingers into the narrow slit, pulling outward. His biceps bulge, his open armpits releasing a strong, pungent smell, slightly fishy. She's seen this routine in cartoons and thriller movies, but, miraculously, he manages to pry the doors open with a little groan. Grey concrete three inches away. No escape.

"We're between floors," he says. "C'mon. Hit that button for fifteen and see what happens." She touches it and the elevator falls one foot.

"Hit it again," he says.

Little by little they fall past the fifteenth floor. The elevator suddenly drops ten feet. Light, the orange carpeting of the hallway, glass mirrors rush by.

"Do it again. Only this time, hit fourteen," he says, excited. They both know now there is a way out, if they're lucky with timing and they work together fluidly, the man yelling "Now!" as he pries the doors open.

"I can see light!" he says. "We're almost there." All his nonchalance is gone. They laugh together, nervously, when the fourteenth floor slips by.

"Let's try for thirteen," he says, looking up to the lighted board above his head. "Where the hell is thirteen?"

"Superstition," she tells him and he smiles as though she's said something witty.

Together, they work the elevator down in little jerks and it falls to a thick bar of light below their feet.

"Do you want to risk taking it all the way?" he asks her.

"No. Let's jump out," Anna replies.

"Go ahead. I'll hold the door," and Anna leaps through the door quickly, knowing that the elevator might slip at any moment and crush her, half in, half out. From dimness to light, from the close dampness of the elevator to the chilled air-conditioned hall. She falls to her knees, gets up, reluctant to look at him still in the elevator, floating halfway up the mirrored wall. Beneath him are the inner concrete walls of the shaft and black cables. He uses all his strength to push the doors as wide as he can and jumps clear before they close behind him.

"Out at last! We'd better go down the stairwell," he says.

The shaking in Anna's legs has turned into a jelled weakness.

"I'd never make it down twelve flights. My legs," she is not ashamed to tell him. "I haven't slept in twenty-two nights," she says impulsively.

"Do you mean you want to get back in?" he asks.

Anna doesn't answer and she sinks to a sitting position.

"You go ahead. I'll wait here," she says.

"We'll just take one of the other elevators. They're not connected," he offers. "We have to go down one floor, anyway. No other elevator will stop." And he smiles at her, waiting, as she wraps her skirt around her and slowly rises to her feet. The stairwell door clanks behind them as in a prison. They pick up momentum going down the concrete stairs; he is taking them two at a time. She tries to keep up, but only meets him again at the elevator on the eleventh floor. He presses the signal. They wait, slightly giddy. The light-hearted mood between them collapses when the broken elevator opens its doors.

"I'm not getting back in that one," she tells him. "Even if it's acting perfectly normal, I'm not getting in."

"Look at that," he says, pointing to the slightly raised floor. "Something is wrong with it for sure." Now that the immediate danger is passed, he seems to see the elevator as a challenge. She senses that he wants to defeat it, that he will not leave her now until they both make it down.

"We've got to get two floors away, then. Up or down?" he asks Anna.

"Down."

They move slowly toward the stairwell. This time she feels uneasy. Why is he sticking with her? Is he waiting for an opportunity? Does he think she owes him something? He's behind her on the stairs, but she slows, pretending to catch her breath so that he'll move ahead of her. She wants him where she can see him.

At the ninth floor, when the same damaged elevator turns up, they are not surprised. She tells him to go ahead, she'll wait for the good one. His face suddenly hardens into wariness.

"You shouldn't be in an elevator alone," he says.

"Why not? That's where I was when you got on," Anna replies, not looking at him.

"Listen, I'm not hassling you. Let's just send this one away, OK? You hold the doors open, I'll reach in and send it back up to the penthouse."

Anna holds the doors, careful to keep her head out of the elevator just in case it plummets again. She remembers a news story from a few years back, a tourist who was decapitated by a falling elevator in a hotel that was under construction. She keeps her head free, but her hands tingle as she holds the doors. She can see herself standing there, stunned, like some grisly saint as her severed hands plummet. The man long gone as well. But he dashes in quickly, presses a button, makes it out unharmed.

"There. That's the last we'll see of that sucker," he says and chuckles a little. They are both surprised when the elevator on the right answers their summons. Still, Anna is reluctant to step over the threshold.

To make amends for her sharpness, she asks, "It couldn't happen again with this one, could it?"

He shrugs as they step on together.

The journey down nine floors to the lobby is smooth and uneventful. The evenness of the hum, the monotony of the passage, gradually turns them into strangers again. The elevator slows once, at the third floor, and the entry of someone who knows nothing of their shared experience is both a relief and a disappointment. They step out into the lobby, heading for the glass doors reflecting their images back at them before they cross into darkness. She realizes that if she doesn't address him, he will say nothing.

"Should I put up a note?" she says.

"Yeah, sure," he says, stopping to hand her a pen unclipped from the pocket of his T-shirt.

She roots through her purse, writes a note, sticks it between the mirrors in the lobby. *Danger. Out of control.* He takes back his pen, reads her note and laughs. She laughs, too, and the connection between them returns. She opens the glass door for him and comments, "I thought you were headed for the basement."

"I changed my mind," he says. "See you."

To change your mind. A simple thing: to step off suddenly one level up, push open glass doors and step out into this fragrant spring night.

DREAM HORSES

Ruth sets across the prairie to reach Iris' clapboard
house, avoiding the dusty reserve road along Cold
Lake. Pregnancy slows her as she follows the path
behind the teachers' trailers, past the empty corral. She
holds her breath as she enters the forest where tree trunks
were stripped by fire several years before. Here the smell
hugging the ground is vaguely familiar. She sips its sweetness
with her nose and feels suddenly dreamy. Miniature leaves
film the sky in a thin ceiling.

She thinks she sees people standing quietly in the low
willows, but it's just the strips of faded cloth tied to branches.
Offerings to the sun. Often she sees horses, grey and pale
brown, far enough away that she can't hear anything of their
movement but the occasional crack of a broken branch under
their hooves, like dream horses, lifting their massive heads to
look at her as they slowly retreat. They frighten her.

It is a relief to reach the edge of prairie. She passes old
homesteads, marked by toppled woodstoves and stairs

leading up to the intense blue sky. Finally she reaches the shade of poplars arcing over the rutted track of Iris' driveway. She knows enough about cultural differences by now to suppress her insecurities. When she first arrived from the city, she felt hurt by the silence of her neighbours. These initial silences will never come naturally to her, but at least she accepts them.

Iris is washing clothes by hand on a washboard in a steel tub. She acknowledges Ruth with a nod, plunges her arms again into soapy water. Ruth sits on a wooden block scarred by an axe and waits. Eventually, Iris says, "Someone hit a horse near Cold Lake last night."

The water pouring from the clothes is reddish.

"Was anyone hurt?" she asks.

"Oh, no. Well, just the horse," Iris says, laughing and leaning back for a minute to rub her back. "Cal and I dragged it into the ditch."

She bends back into her washing and the tips of her braids dip into the bloody water.

"Iris, your braids," she says, startled. She is dazed by the up-and-down scrubbing against the washboard.

"Just hold them back. I'm almost finished."

Ruth stands behind her, the two black braids in her hands. She forgets to move with her and Iris' head jerks back.

"Ouch," she says, laughing.

"Sorry. I keep dozing off."

"You walked across the prairie to get here? That's a long way in your condition," Iris says over her shoulder as she walks with the basin toward the clothesline. She pins the two shirts to the line. The stains blossom in the wind. "Not much hope for those, eh?" she says. "Let's have some tea. It'll wake you up."

They sit inside. Ruth looks around the room at all the strange objects that don't seem to belong together: crucifixes, beaded and feathered hair ornaments, a velvet painting of a bullfight hung next to a Union Jack. She sits quietly, transfixed by a pastoral calendar from a butcher shop in Saskatoon. Spots float across her field of vision. The baby is a magnet pulling all the blood out of her head.

An accordion with two pearly panels lurches to one side. Out of the corner of her eye, she sees it opening and closing ever so slightly, breathing.

"You must wish you were going home to have the baby. Is your mother coming soon?" Iris asks.

"No." She pauses. "My mother would be totally bushed here."

Iris sits quietly, a look of sympathy or suspicion. She feels uncomfortable telling her about her own upper class suburban upbringing. Iris is from the Poorman reserve. She almost winced when Iris first mentioned it, but Ruth doesn't think anything of it now. It's just a place name. Just like the last names of the students in Martin's class: Starchild and Snakeskin and Flyingdust.

"My father was shot," Iris told her matter of factly one day. "We were riding bareback. It's strange, I heard it after we fell to the ground." Ruth didn't know what to say, so she sat quietly as she was learning to do.

"I used to drink, just like him. Until I met Cal and we went into rehab."

Ruth could have said, "My father drank, too. He's dead now," but she didn't, or couldn't, and the moment passed. Some test of friendship had been failed, yet she still walks to see Iris on long Saturday afternoons when Martin is catching up on marking, bringing a book for her or a message because the school has one of the only telephones on the reserve. Iris makes her taste the dust of Poorman. The long silences between them fill effortlessly and the tight spot in her chest relaxes just a little. Without such excursions she feels totally lost.

She knows Martin is grounded here. In the evenings, he is attentive to his work, bending over his desk, a bright light trained on loose-leaf paper, rearranging phrases, filling in verb tenses and punctuation. Each tick of his red pen is an affirmation. When Ruth met him, he seemed so free, so willing to spend the nights reading poetry to her. They drifted together through a winter like that and she felt an airiness for the first time since her father's death.

Then he took her to the farm where he grew up and she saw the tilted outbuildings, the rocky land of the Canadian Shield jutting through the fields gone to weed since his father's death. His mother held her hand too tightly, too desperately. Only recently has she been able to identify what was so familiar about the reserve. But Martin could do here what he couldn't at home. Here, he could extend his hand, pull with whatever force was necessary if someone grabbed on. Both Iris and Cal were in his class and it was Cal whom Martin mentioned at night with a kind of intense fascination. It was Cal, in a way, who was responsible for Iris' friendship with Ruth.

Iris had knocked on the door of her trailer late one afternoon and introduced herself.

"Martin thought you needed some company. Cal's got him all fired up about *Hamlet* and we're going to have to wait a long, long time," she laughed, quick and wry.

Once they settled into a comfortable rhythm, Ruth asked her, "What is it Cal likes about *Hamlet*?"

"Family troubles. All those ghosts. If the two of them start talking about ghosts, we'll be here all night. Cal has a million ghost stories."

"What about you?"

"Ghosts or *Hamlet*?"

"*Hamlet*, I guess. Did you like the play?"

Iris shuddered. "When they're digging up skulls and Hamlet picks it up, talking about who it was, that was too much for me."

Ruth thought of Martin at his father's grave the summer before. She remembered how edgy he had been when he finally agreed to take her to the little churchyard where his father was buried. She had squatted and leaned back on her heels, her hand tracing the letters of his father's name, a man she had never met. She read each family stone carefully as he said, "C'mon. Let's get going."

"Why? When were you last here?"

"The last time I was here, I dug that grave. With my brothers," he said. "No hired help for the poor."

She looked at Iris now and picked up the thread of their conversation. "And what about ghosts?"

"I live in the here and now," she said and in the months since Ruth has known her she has come to see this is true of Iris.

"I'll go home next Christmas," Ruth lies today.

"I couldn't last that long without seeing my mother. She's looking after my kids. We're going down to get them now that we're ready."

"Things aren't that easy with my mother. She's very busy," she says, retreating. "She's a doctor."

"You must have been rich! And now you're stuck here with the rest of us."

"I like it here. I really do," Ruth says. Ruth wonders what it is about Iris that pulls Ruth out where she isn't sure she wants to go. She studies Iris' beautiful cheekbones, her thin hips, the way she bends to pick up wood before hurling it into the woodstove, her long braids swinging. She is like her namesake, slender, firm, delicate and strong. But no one has flower gardens here.

"You look really tired. Why don't you take a nap? Cal can drive you home later."

Ruth slips gratefully to the couch, placing her head next to the accordion. The house is quiet after Iris carries another basket of laundry outside. Faster than she could have imagined, she is dreaming. The marble panel of the accordion becomes the impervious slab of a tall building. She drifts down onto the concrete of a city street, onto a sidewalk she recognizes. A tall office building stretches a city block beside her. It changes colour, becomes a sandy red and she recognizes the office where both her parents practised medicine when she was young. They are up there, some-where, behind serene glass, as clouds tear apart and shred on the edges of the building.

"We'd better go," she hears her mother whisper. "I'll walk with you."

She wakes to the sound of a man slurring and yelling outside. It's Cal.

"Machinery. Stupid machinery ..." A dull thud of a boot hitting metal. "... not worth a goddamn." Hubcaps ring out and spin on gravel.

"Iris?" he shouts. "Where are your keys?"

Ruth's legs buckle under her as she trips down the back steps. Iris pulls her up and leads her quietly down a trail through the poplars. Beside them, a long line of wrecked cars, parked or abandoned, reflect just enough light from the open kitchen door to keep them on the path. A motor sits glistening on the hood of a car. Ruth recoils from its unexpected shape.

"He takes most of it out on the car. *Most* of it," Iris says. She's awake now, alert. She realizes that she has never looked closely at Cal, hasn't seen past his glasses, trained on his schoolbooks as though his life depended on it.

"Does he come home like that a lot?" Ruth finally asks when they turn onto the dirt road. They slow their pace. The night is dark as deep water.

"Just when he's with his family."

"You don't go with him?"

"They think I'm stuck up. Keep asking him what's

wrong with the women on this reserve that he had to go south to find one."

Then Ruth knows something she wouldn't have thought, misled as she is by Iris' braids and easy manner. Iris is an outsider here, too.

Ruth feels something hit her chest in soft waves. Pregnancy fills her body with unfamiliar sensations that disorient her and dissolve her borders so that she can't always tell what is outside and what is inside, but Iris grabs her hand.

"Listen!" Iris pulls her to a stop, her fingernails cutting into her palm. The road beneath their feet is shaking, then a low distant rolling, not a shock wave, not thunder.

"Horses! On the road, coming at us!" Iris yells. Ruth wrenches her hand away and runs sideways, blinded and panicking in darkness. She wants to find the ditch, some indentation, no matter how shallow, and curl herself into the smallest shape she can.

"No! Don't hide. They have to be able to see you! They can see in the dark better than we can." She hears Iris' voice pitched high, a wail headed away from her and toward the oncoming stampede.

Iris claps her hands and screams at the approaching horses, "Go! Get out of the way! Go away!" And before either of them even identifies what is coming at them, the horses veer suddenly onto the prairie, the booming recedes and they are gone.

In the hospital after her son is born, the old nightmares return. She dreams that she and her father are standing on a platform watching a satellite revolve. She dreams they are part of a silent crowd in an airport. Through curved glass, the hull of a plane looms closer and closer. Before glass shatters, she wakes with a small, suppressed cry. Sometimes there is a shape standing in the doorway, backlit. A voice soothing her, "It's OK. It's just your milk coming in." The nurse is gone before she is fully conscious.

This was her father's domain. He walked the hallways of hospitals like a feudal lord, the sweet chloroform stench of the air clinging to his clothes when he came into her room late at night. She imagined it was the smell of healing, of deep, painless sleep, not the sweet vapours of liquor. She would pretend she was asleep; that way he would stay longer, looking down on her. When she remembers him now it is from a distance. He is striding purposefully away down long corridors, his voice booming and echoing across large rooms.

Then, suddenly, he no longer looked down on her at night. One night, her mother's nurse came instead, wrapped her and carried her through the lit house where the heavy boots of policemen sounded up and down the basement stairs. They looked away from her as she was carried sleepily down the wide front hall, through the open door, past the ambulance gleaming beside the gold carriage lamp. On the way through the house, she heard her mother's calm voice questioning the policemen.

Such a night of sorrow had been a night of pleasure at the time. Her mother's nurse stroked her forehead as she lay on the leather couch in her mother's office, sang to her, tucked around her the quilt from her bed at home. What a strange and magical morning it had been, awakening to sweet Danish on a paper plate and real tea. She never saw her father again.

The nurse in this small prairie hospital fills her with the same sense of gratitude. Each time she brings the baby in the middle of the night, everything clicks into focus and the strange hollowness of her empty body dissolves into the fullness she holds in her arms. The nurse smiles at the tears she tries to hide by turning her face away.

"Some women feel like this after they've had a baby. It's normal," she says. The nurse reaches down casually and strokes her engorged breast.

"Just let the milk come," she says, holding the nipple between two fingers. "Here, now let him fasten on," and Ruth feels the heat prickling, rushing down and out her nipples. The baby pulls back, surprised, then roots in again with renewed determination. They both laugh. Though when the nurse leaves, carrying the baby under one arm, the terrible loneliness settles upon her like a dark weight. No one else reaches into this private world, not her husband, not the voices on the phone calling from her distant, now irrelevant past.

Her mother's voice melts into a blur of medical details. "Demerol?" she asks. "That's all they had to offer you? What kind of a primitive hospital are you in?"

A cloaked criticism, she knows from experience, of Martin, for taking her away, bringing her here. She slept through her father's funeral, thanks to her mother's injection.

None of it matters now. The baby brings the fever of her

emotions up and down. A terrible hushed love, the fear that he will lie in her arms forever, or the fear that he will slip away. When he isn't connected to her flesh, she can't sleep. The nurse shadows all these shifts of feeling and, in turn, Ruth picks up her moods, even when words don't pass between them.

The nurse comes to her room on the last afternoon, lifts the baby with a closed, pursed expression. She smiles then, as usual, and says, "Someone wants to see you. She says she's a friend." Ruth hears the rest as though it is spoken out loud, "But how could she be?"

Iris steps by the nurse, who presses herself against the door as Iris passes by.

"You need to rest before you go home, so not too long," the nurse says to Ruth.

Iris pulls a chair close to Ruth's bed and sits down heavily. Ruth notices that her skin is dusky, almost purplish. She sighs and a whiff of sweet fermentation riffles over Ruth's face, making her stiffen.

"Heh, how's it going?"

"Oh, you know. You've been through it."

"Well, it stops hurting fast enough. You got the blues yet?"

"No. I'll have lots to do once I get home. No time for the blues," Ruth says, despising how clipped and efficient her own voice sounds.

Iris understands at once. She looks down, embarrassed, then remembers something. She reaches into a cloth bag and holds out a soft handful of deerskin.

"Your baby's first home is a reserve. He should have a moss bag."

"That's beautiful, Iris. Thank you." And it is beautiful, the soft narrow sack in her hands with its careful geometric beadwork in watery shades of blue and green.

"You should be studying, not sewing," she says.

"The only way to get ahead in this world, eh?"

The nurse looks around the doorframe, but before she has a to chance to say anything, Iris gets up to leave.

"Guess you won't be dropping by much anymore," she says.

"It's your turn to do the walking," Ruth says. But she knows Iris will never come.

Cold Lake stretches grey and still to her right as they drive back from the city. Since the baby was born, she longs for both crowds and anonymity. They often drive to North Battleford so she can stand in an aisle at Woolworth's, mesmerized by the reflected light of hundreds of glasses on shelves. Every time they drive back to the reserve, the darkness settles in earlier. Each little town, eight miles from the next one, rises up in brooding grain elevators and sinks again in a small cluster of lights. The reserve is a dark pool they turn towards.

She dreads the winter ahead. The lake has receded, cold already thickening the water, and white rings of minerals lie along the shore. Those same rings appear on her shirts and dark sweaters between feedings. All that slow seeping, a painless wound, milk that seems to ease out of her heart.

She leaves the lights off when she sits in the living room of their trailer during night feedings. The baby snuffles close to her skin and Ruth wonders how long she can prolong this sensation of safety for her son. She is vigilant now; she can't sleep. During these feedings, she thinks of her father, remembering the safety conveyed by his voice on the phone in another room. For years, she hasn't been able to remember his voice, but now she can, sitting up in the middle of the night, thousands of miles and many years away from his grave.

Stray dogs wander in the schoolyard, barking. They start to gather again now that the wind is cold at night, howling off the prairie. When she looks up at the window, she sees the shadows of two men creased in the curtains. The heads duck and she hears a knocking on the outside of the trailer and a sound like hair being torn out. The heads rise again and peer in. Her heart races, she gathers her baby closer and is about to call out for Martin when the heads turn sideways and she sees their long snouts. Wild horses, eating the grass that still grows at the base of the trailer. The sound of ripping grass goes on and on, but there is no use chasing them away.

RED BECOMES RED

Quill. Even her name hurts me, a hook in my heart. It was a private joke. She broke the water inside me so I imagined her holding something sharp and wild in her hand, choosing the moment to be born. The three of us — mother, father and child — slept while the midwife sat in a chair beside us, watching for storm clouds. The angel passed over. Then I rose, left them there asleep, and when the moon lifted in the sky, went with the midwife to the garden to plant the afterbirth. It had cooled slightly, a slippery, spineless sea creature that swam away from me, leaping out of my hands before the hole was deep enough.

"Plant your tomatoes here. You'll have the sweetest crop," she said.

"Red becomes red," I said, filled with such thankfulness. Stars swirled above me. I was still a bit faint.

But now she's like a squirming black dog clamped

between my legs as I pull quills out with pliers before they work themselves into the brain. Quills can drive a dog mad.

A year has passed and finally I can say her name, though still not to him. The door fans inward, he brings a gust of air so cold I think it has frozen into this blinding light. I turn away just after I catch that look on his face. His eyes, watchful, bluer than they used to be, as though the water that drowned her is rising up inside him. I've seen him sweep it away with the back of his knuckle. A man's tears are always furtive.

He steps out of his work boots, walks toward me with the empty ice cream pail and places it on the counter. I'm sitting and smoking, still in my housecoat. I started smoking again when the cold weather came. I wanted that desert burn in my throat.

"The chickens have stopped laying again. Only one egg," he says. "Here, it's warm." He reaches to place the egg, still smeared with straw and shit, in my hand.

The cold that swept in with him raises goose bumps on my thigh where my legs are crossed. I shift away from him before the ugly thing is in my hand, lift the edge of the housecoat and cover my leg. He turns away from me, keeping his face set in angry profile, a beard of stone, so that I'll know he's taken this personally.

"Don't they have enough light?" I ask.

He dissolves and his attention rushes back towards me.

"Not in this cold. And, Rachel, I mean cold. When's the last time you were outside?"

I leave my smouldering cigarette, a small light of comfort in the wilderness, and move to the window. The backyard blurs into the prairie behind, one undulating expanse of snow. At this time in the morning, the light doesn't separate snow from sky, both go on forever, but it's better than being in town where the chimneys, comings and goings of cars, trucks, people, leave everything enshrouded in a cloud of icy fog. During spells like this, you have to wear a scarf over your mouth to keep the ice crystals from scarring your lungs.

"Looks like a desert. Looks like sand."

"Don't," he says and walks out to his truck, sputtering miserably to life. He backs out without disconnecting the extension for the block heater. The bright orange cord pulls taut, then snaps. Now, he'll have something else to keep him occupied. Good for him.

Polydipsia: sustained excessive thirst, the kind of thirst that drives you to drink anything. *Uriposia:* the drinking of urine. *Hemoposia:* the drinking of blood. Words like this rise up like small dead things, gleaming sickly white, in the middle of the night. I hang onto them once I've found them in books and even though they are dead, they buoy me. They are better than the smothering nothing I nudged up against for the first couple of months. Better than the vision that troubles me now, blindsiding me with its uselessness. At first, the visions were fractured: the blinding glare of head-lights, Quill turning her face away as though she saw it coming. Always she dove down deeper in the lake than any-one else. And always she returned, grinning and squinting in the sun, shivering as I wrapped a towel around her.

"Where've you been?" I asked.

"To the other side of the world," she said. "You should see it, Mom. I love it down there."

"In my dreams, sweet pea. You know I'm not a swimmer."

But I never dreamed of water, only rain.

In the winter, we slept till after nine, the light easing to silver, then brightening through the white lace curtains in our bedroom like radioactive milk.

Quill, even as a toddler, would wake before me. Perhaps it was the sound of Michael stoking up the wood furnace in the cellar that woke her.

When I awoke, she would be lying beside me, pale brown eyes so large in her small face. The pillow sank beneath her and it occurred to me that her head had weight, was full of her own thoughts.

I yawned and put my arm across her small shoulders.

"What are you looking at, Quill?"

"I'm watching you dream," she said.

"How do you know I'm dreaming?"

"I can see," she said and looked at the ceiling. "Up there. There were trees across the road. They fell down."

And she was right. I had been dreaming of black skies opening in a torrent of rain and the prairie ground shifting, sliding into impossible mud. The shallow roots of poplars lining the narrow roads were losing their grip and toppled with gusts of wind.

This terrified me the first time it really happened, in the early months of my pregnancy. It had rained all night. The air, usually gritty in my nose, was thick, smelled of tears, the salt in the soil dissolving into the wet air. Michael could hardly wait to start the four-wheel drive.

"Put your seat belt on. We're going for a ride," though he didn't fasten his own. He slid the truck from shoulder to shoulder, leaving yellow ruts in the mud behind us. We rounded the curve and slid suddenly sideways when he saw the downed poplar across the road.

I dreamed this over and over, trees losing their footing both in front and behind us, the roads even more impassable in summer than in winter. I was afraid of being blocked from the hospital, so Michael found the name of a midwife from the back-to-the-land community near Willow Lake.

"If Mohammed cannot go to the mountain, then the mountain will come to Mohammed," he said.

The dreams stopped once the midwife arrived. Jessie, her light brown hair springing from a red scarf, made good soups and was generous with backrubs and easy prophecies.

"This is a strong baby, a strong heart," she said, with the stethoscope pressed against my belly. "This one wants to live."

Just before labour started, Michael and I sat in the truck. It was four in the morning and we were near the community pasture. He held a beer between his thighs. The baby was so big, I felt like someone was sitting on my knee. I could see the brush piles on fire across the newly cleared field. Jets of orange sparks sprayed up when the breeze lifted.

For weeks, these fires smouldered by day and flickered by night, like northern lights snagged in these piles of poplar. The more prosperous farmers had bought up old fields left fallow, were reclaiming them from rough bush, bulldozing trees into piles and letting fire do most of the work. Through those nights in August, the glow in the sky from three sides drew us out when we couldn't sleep. We were protected by a ring of fire.

It seemed prophetic, the way it started, a sudden soaking gush of salty warmth beneath me as we watched the flames. Fire and water. We would be blessed for life.

Michael rocks against me in his sleep. It's a feeling like seasickness, his neediness, his radar even when he's unconscious. If I turned towards him, he would envelop me in an instant. Thirst gets me out of bed, draws me, parched, toward the stained bathroom sink. The water here is drawn to the surface so painfully, it's tinged with blood. And it stinks. When I first came here from the city, he tasted like it. His kiss seemed like the kiss of an impostor. He noticed my shyness.

"It's the water. What's the human body, ninety-eight percent water? Give yourself a few weeks and you won't notice a thing. Your skin," and he kissed my forehead. "Your brain, watery mush. Soon all you'll want is sex, day and night."

"Don't you wish."

"Your breasts will fill up," and he started to undo the top buttons of my shirt.

Now he is a stranger again, and I stand with a glass of tinged water in my hand, unable to drink. I've forgotten how. The muscles in my throat tense, my breathing comes in ragged bursts. I can take only a few sips. The simple rhythmic pleasure is gone. Yet, I'm always thirsty.

For the longest time, the first and last postcard she ever sent us was on the fridge. On the way to Edmonton to visit the West Edmonton Mall, the school bus stopped in Vegreville for lunch, near the giant Ukrainian painted egg. On the front of the card is the egg, with intricate and bright designs, tilted a little to the side against an intense blue sky. Her message is half printed, half written: "This egg is as big as a dinosaur! As big as the whole world! I love you. Quill." Her name is cursive, slanted a little like the egg, with glimmerings of the person she will become, the quickly dashed hand of a woman on the move. There is an eraser smudge on the word "whole" and I can see beneath it that she had originally written "hole."

The card arrived the week we buried her in the Turtle Lake cemetery. I didn't get out of the car. The dirt heaped in the snow looked obscene, looked like a pile of shit. Michael grabbed my leg just above the knee, hard, said, "We've got to. We owe it to her."

"No. You go."

"And if I don't, who does?"

I didn't answer. Other people were there, but we couldn't see them. It was as though they had become ghosts while Quill was still very real. Ghost faces, ghost friends, ghost family calling long distance. By then, our breath had frozen on the windshield of the minister's car. I couldn't see the pile of shit anymore, but I heard frozen dirt rattle viciously on the top of her box and then a heavier sound as the earth filled in, a dull thud like the sound of geese hitting the ground after they're shot.

Michael came back to the car, the shape of him blurry and dark against the silvery frost of the windows, holding on inside until he closed the car door. That heaving grief, like being sick. I floated inside my head, wanting to drift into the cold, cold blue.

"You wanted her to go to school," I said. "I could have taught her at home, but you wanted her to go to school."

I went to the church one more time after that. I sat at the back so that the sunlight cutting through the narrow windows wouldn't fall on me. A few aboriginal grand-mothers sat near me with purple kerchiefs over their hair. One smiled slightly and nodded her head as I slipped into the pew beside her. They know what it's like. Children are always dying out on the reserve, in house fires, in cars stuck in snowdrifts. I hear these things and carry them around with me, as they must carry my loss with them. I lie in bed making comparisons, shopping for a more bearable kind of grief. Everyone in the church was old. The white women all sat in front of me, their hair silvery variations on blue under fur hats. They went all the way to Saskatoon for these hats, years ago, just after the war. They wouldn't know what to do if someone from the reserve placed the bloody skins in their hands, fresh from the trap.

The gospel was from Matthew. An angel appeared to Joseph in a dream and told him to flee to Egypt because Herod would destroy him. In his anger at Jesus' escape, Herod killed all the children under three. I'd heard enough. I got up to leave. Then I heard my name. God was speaking to me, as he'd refused to before. I would have listened then. He could have warned me. But not now. Not ever again.

In the morning, Michael is gone. His absence is welcome. Once, late last winter, he almost made me see what I didn't want to see. He arrived at dawn, after walking all night, all the way from Turtle Lake. His truck was marooned out in the snow on the frozen lake. He slipped into bed beside me, still wrapped in the smell of fresh air, and put his arms around me, his chest against me making me shiver. He told me the moonlight was so beautiful on the lake that he revved the truck, took a run at it and sailed far out into the fluffy, trackless snow. It sprayed up around him sparkling, bouncing off his windshield before he came to rest sixty feet from shore.

"You know what, Rachel? It was worth it." And for a moment I saw the light lifting and the pristine lake unbroken, something of the possibility of beauty in the world without her.

But I turned over, told him to plug in the old Volvo, to drive over to Hurdman's farm for the tractor. I didn't want to go with him. He got here on his own. He could go back alone for all I cared.

I lie in bed smoking, watching it flower in the air above me. The fluted shape of blue lilies blooming and wilting in the air. I slip down low in the bed and see what isn't. What is, what was, I had to leave behind.

The Sands Hotel, which we never saw. Quill caught by her bathing suit on the drain at the bottom of the hotel pool. I used to see her thrashing, the legs of the others far above her, near light, taking those first lungfuls of water, relaxing a little because she can breathe as she did before she was born. A miracle, she can breathe under water, and she can hardly wait to tell me. But there are no miracles. God is silent.

I see this instead: Quill and her husband and their six-year-old boy are traveling in the desert. They are driving a Volvo through Egypt, out into the Sahara. She likes the feeling of moving out into extremity. She has never felt more alive. The sand around them is braided and hard. Her teeth rattle in her head when they hit a ripple. Her son is in the back seat; I cannot see him clearly. I only know her love for him as part of the great heart-line passed from mother to child, from me to him through her. Her husband is gentle, a rough-looking gypsy who cherishes her. A man much like her father.

He says to her, "Would you like to drive for a while? I'm getting sleepy." This is well past the turn of the millennium. The desert hasn't changed, will never change. If anything, it has gathered its forces, its ancient Biblical forces, and has smothered small village oases, date palm groves, dissolving mud houses back into a nothingness and driving people back into war with their neighbours. Far beneath the surface are aquifers full of fossil water, from the time when seas covered this continent. Quill feels the presence of these waters in her blood, sees their waves floating above the surface of the horizon.

"Sure," she says.

"Just follow the tracks and we should cross the border by dawn."

Their son is already asleep. Wood bangles she bought in the market in Alexandria slide down her forearm, creating a warm hollow music as he and his father sleep. The mischievous pointed face I know so well has moulded into a face more feral and wise. The sun sinks quickly, lighting up the drifts of sand and hard rock golden-orange, sinking to rose like a fire deepening its embers. Blue slides up from the other horizon and it is suddenly dark. Quill stops the car to step out into the air, filling her lungs. It is like drinking cool water. Stars float to the surface of the sky in torrents. The suddenness of it makes her a bit faint. She thinks of that old-fashioned word "swoon." She's swooning with the beauty of the desert at night. She's thankful to be alive.

She drives all night. Now and then she feels a soft sinking feeling under the car, drifts a little sideways as in a boat, but manages to find hard ground again and carries on. The braided tracks are caused by other vehicles bogged down in sand. People swerve to get around them and the pattern continues for what looks like infinity. She's been told the tracks are ten kilometres wide in places.

He wakes near dawn, a pale rose lid lifting in the east, and behind it the fierce sun, witness of everything that moves below. The sun's attention is too much. He checks maps.

"Did you see a line of rocky cliffs off to your right?"

"We've passed so many rocks," she says. Their son wakes and tells them he needs to pee. They both hold each other back, tense, as they watch his clear water seep into the sand and disappear. They wonder if they should have found an empty canteen to save it, but they're not yet ready to admit what they both know.

"C'mon, hon. The sun's hot. Back in the car," Quill says. She passes him an orange, some dates and unleavened bread. He eats, gazing out the tinted window, still half-claimed by his dream of a narrow country road lined with poplar, throwing a red ball for a black dog. Dreams of home. Dreams of me, his grandmother, at the door calling his name. "Ishmael. Ishmael, come in. Aren't you cold yet?" my voice carrying across the snow.

When the sun is highest in the sky, they run out of gas. They sit silently in the car until the heat drives them out into the desert and then under the car in a shallow dugout where there is shade. Quill squints as she does when focusing her long-distance vision, lifting her sharp chin slightly as though she's sniffing something on the breeze. She waits for a glint on a windshield.

Near sundown, their son begins to cry.

"It's really important that you're strong and that you don't cry. OK?" Quill says, putting her arm around him, her lips to his cheek. She tastes his tears and keeps her mouth there until he's stopped. Then she realizes what she has been doing. *I'm a ghoul, not a mother*, she thinks.

When the water runs out, she gives him his own urine to drink and as much of hers as he can take.

"Yours is too strong for him," she tells her husband. "Keep your own strength up. I'm going to need you."

"Then you have it," he says, holding out his jar of dark yellow fluid.

"No, you," Quill says, pushing it back.

They push the jar back and forth till they finally laugh. Quill's heart beats hard. She knows it is the last laugh they will ever share.

On the third day, he digs a trench below the engine, moving slowly because he is so fatigued. He brings back radiator coolant in a clear glass jar, bright green, which makes her head hurt just to look at it. The fluid seems to gel in the hot sun, like green blood, but it's just an illusion.

"It's not so bad," she tells him, taking her first mouthful

Still, it's just as well that their son is beyond drinking now. He lies in the shallow bowl of sand under the car, breathing fast, his skin thinning like an old man's. She sits beside him, stroking his forehead. For a while he whined and tried to sweep her hand away, but he no longer makes a sound.

Talking is difficult for her, too, but she says to her husband, "This is familiar somehow. I've been here before."

"No. We would never have come back," her husband says. "If only we'd known."

"But I know this place. I've done this before. I swear."

Their son hallucinates. He tries to cry out, but his voice crackles in his throat. His tongue is swelling. How she does it, or exactly when, she doesn't record. She writes on maps, first on the edges and borders to preserve them, then on top of lines and little points of settlements when it doesn't matter anymore. I will be given these maps. After many months, or maybe years, I will find them in my hands.

"He's out of pain. I feel nothing," she writes.

She's alone now. After they stop their son's breathing and cover him with silky sand, her husband lifts his wrist, tells her, "Drink. You still have a chance." And to her shame, she does, through a slit he's made in his forearm, but the blood doesn't flow quickly enough. It is so thick. He holds his chin up as he lies beside her and she cuts through and drinks. Before he has even stopped breathing, she throws up red in the sand. It dries quickly and is lifted by the wind.

"I don't regret coming here," she writes. "The desert is so powerful, so beautiful. I only regret it's not an easier death, a cool and soothing death. I long to drown."

And I'm back where I begin.

The package of cigarettes is empty, so I rise. I put my parka on over my housecoat and go outside to the chicken

coop we fashioned from an old garden shed. The air is so
cold I gasp, then reach down to zip up the front and find
gloves in my pockets. My eyes are watering, then freezing
my eyelashes together in a line of ice. A musty smell inside
the coop hints of summer. The hens are on their perches,
dark feathers puffed up, heads tucked under flightless
wings. Their quiet female broodiness used to be such a
comfort to me, but now it feels like a reproach. Quill loved
them, especially when we first brought them home, peeping
in a box, growing in the dark under blood-red lights.

"Can I sit with them here, Mom?"

"Sit too long under this magic light and *you'll* start laying
eggs," I told her, struck by the picture of her with her own
child someday.

I reach into box after box of straw, sweep around with
my gloved hand, finding nothing.

This is not a choice I make, but a kind of certainty. I step
out into the fenced-in chicken run, clear off the wide
stump, open our little tool shed and find what I need.

I choose one furthest from the door. The bird quivers
warm in my hands, a few misfired impulses to fly, before
settling against my stomach. Once we reach the light, I grab
its feet, swing it out in front of me the way I've seen
Michael do and with one quick arc of axe on wood, its head
falls to the ground. The hen jerks out of my hands, beating
wings convulsively, making thin trails of blood, loopy handwriting, in the snow. I go back for the next and the next.
It's so cold, blood freezes like glue on my cheek, freezes
into little pellets underfoot. I throw the hens' bodies in a
small pile. The pot should be boiling so that they can be

dipped and the dark feathers will come clean from the shocking white flesh.

Arms clamp me from behind. The axe head brushes my boot.

"You've snapped. You've really snapped," Michael shouts in my ear. I can't get loose so I try to bite his arm. His jacket is too thick.

"Are you ready to stop now?" He flings me away from him.

I've come to rest close to the chickens. The feathers ruffle slightly in the air, but the birds are inert as brown stones.

"Why don't you just tear out my heart? Will that be enough blood shed for you?"

The word floats up from the carnage. "*Hemoposia*," I say.

"What?"

"I did this," I tell him. "This was something I could do."

We prepared the chickens together. We went through the motions, salvaging something, stripping what was once living down to meat and bone. He was no longer angry. I dipped the bodies in boiling water, held them for a minute, then lifted them out to pluck them on newspaper. Feathers stuck, soft and cloying, to my wet hands. Then he gutted the birds, the smell, humid as sex, wafting up between us.

"It's OK, Rachel. They don't feel a thing now."

Then he passed them back to me so I could rinse and pluck the last stubborn quills. It is a familiar act, passing bodies warm and yielding from hand to hand, like washing a newborn.

"Quill," I said. He kept working, but I sensed a pause, a holding of breath.

"Do you ever wonder?" I ask him. "Wonder how they touched her? Did they even know her name?" I said.

"I don't know what you mean," he said.

"She was naked at the hospital. Who took off her bathing suit? Was it when she was being saved or when they'd given up?"

"Maybe the nurse. She seemed pretty shaken up."

"What was she wearing? What did she wear in the coffin?"

"I bought her a dress in town. Actually, they gave it to me. It was plaid, Blackwatch I think. And Iris, from the reserve, gave me moccasins, for her journey, she said."

"Thank you, Michael. I can't remember a thing, except that her hair was dry. Not a mark on her. It didn't make sense."

"No, it doesn't."

Michael said he needed to clear his head. He's cutting wood in the forest north of the house, as he always does this time of year. The trees are new-growth poplar and birch that have grown on the fields cleared briefly in the Thirties. People built quick, slanting houses, like the one we live in now, then walked away when their real home, their real fields down south came back to life after the dust settled.

Michael loves this land and everything about it. Sometimes he puts his chain saw down and leans against the cold, grey skin of a poplar, looking up at the sky, swaying the tree with his body. I've come upon him unexpectedly, when Quill and I used to take afternoon walks in the forest. He would look surprised and come over to us, lifting Quill in his arms. He usually had something wonderful to show her: the place where deer had slept, flattening the grass; a wasps' nest high in a tree; coyote tracks along the creek.

It's the feeling that he's out there somewhere holding her in his arms that has me pulling on my boots, finding my hat and down-filled mitts and pulling on my parka, still smeared with chicken blood. The sun and cold slap me in the face but instead of waking me up, the blow leaves me dazed, as though the past year may not have really happened and she's out there. This is the first time I've felt released from her terrible absence.

I turn away from the prairie into the bush and hear a dry creaking of wood as two branches scrape together over my head. The air is so cold it is almost electric, so cold it feels like intense heat, as though the bare treetops could burst into flames. I walk by the slough and imagine the frogs frozen solid, not even the core of the earth is warm enough to touch them. And Quill, I do not imagine her physical form now, knowing through the whole restless, seething summer that she had entered the cycle of life in a terrible way. It's easier now that she, too, is frozen, held in a pause.

The clearing is ahead of me. The light seems fierce. My forehead is starting to pound from the cold. I don't hear the chain saw. Still, I know he's there.

I find him inside a ring of trees. He is a dark shape, almost invisible. His boot prints loop in circles, sawdust ground into the snow. I could trace his steps and find out where he's been, in what order and how this happened, but it's random, really. It makes no difference. There are tangles of branches from the high tops of poplar trees, silver as steel wool. He seems very still, but as I get closer I see that he's shivering violently and the skin around his eyes and mouth is blue. He lies pinned under branches and a trunk. The bark is torn and shredded above him. At first I think he has done this with his bare hands, with his nails, but then I notice the axe beside him.

He doesn't seem to realize I'm here. I free the axe and hack away some of the smaller branches. Then I find a reserve of strength and somehow lift the tree, letting it fall beside him. He opens his eyes.

I unzip his parka. He turns his head away. He will not look me in the eye. I open my coat, lie down on top of him, curling his arms inward so that his hands are locked under my arms, chest to chest. His heart is beating too fast. His shivers almost shake me off and after a while he winces.

"My lungs," he says, his voice high and quiet, like the one he will have as an old man. "I think I've collapsed a lung."

I shift so that my weight is lower. The colour slowly changes in his face. I'm eager for it, thirsty for it, the blood rising from his heart. We lie like this for a long time, tears freezing on my face, before I can help him home.

ACKNOWLEDGEMENTS

I would like to thank the members of my Ottawa writers' group for offering honest and astute criticism of early drafts of many of these stories. I would especially like to thank Gabriella Goliger, Susan Zettell and Vivian Tors for reading stories more than once, Sandra Nicholls, for reading the manuscript as a whole, and Joy Gugeler, my editor at Raincoast Books, for streamlining my words into their final form. Thanks as well to Jim Waite for giving perspective to stories outside my own experience. As always, Tim, Owen and Nadia inspire, encourage and sustain me. I would also like to acknowledge the support of the Regional Municipality of Ottawa-Carleton and the Canada Council for financial support during the writing of this book.

Some of these stories have been published in slightly different forms: "Bloodlines" (formerly "The Human Chain") in *Coming Attractions;* "Claiming the Body" in *The Canadian Forum* and *Coming Attractions;* "Dream Horses" in *Windsor Review;* "Homewrecker" in *Grain;* "Pitiless" (formerly "A Feather from Heaven") in *The Malahat Review;* "Red Becomes Red" in *Quintet;* "Silent Sister" in *Canadian Fiction* and *Carrying Fire: New Fiction Writers;* "Strange Visitors" (formerly "Animate Ghosts") in *Event* and *Revisioning Nature;* "The Lotus-Eater" in *The New Quarterly* and *Coming Attractions;* "Twenty-Two Nights" in *Quarry* and *Vital Signs: New Women Writers.*

OTHER RAINCOAST FICTION

Tracing Iris **by Genni Gunn**
1-55192-486-2 $21.95 CDN $15.95 US

Sounding the Blood **by Amanda Hale**
1-55192-484-6 $21.95 CDN $15.95 US

Small Accidents **by Andrew Gray**
1-55192-508-7 $19.95 CDN $14.95 US

Write Turns: New Directions in Canadian Fiction
1-55192-402-1 $24.95 CDN $19.95 US

Slow Lightning **by Mark Frutkin**
1-55192-406-4 $21.95 CDN $16.95 US

After Battersea Park **by Jonathan Bennett**
1-55192-408-0 $21.95 CDN $16.95 US

Kingdom of Monkeys **by Adam Lewis Schroeder**
1-55192-404-8 $19.95 CDN 14.95 US

Finnie Walsh **by Steven Galloway**
1-55192-372-6 $21.95 CDN $16.95 US

Hotel Paradiso **by Gregor Robinson**
1-55192-358-0 $21.95 CDN $16.95 US

Rhymes with Useless **by Terence Young**
1-55192-354-8 $18.95 cdn $14.95 us

Song of Ascent **by Gabriella Goliger**
1-55192-374-2 $18.95 cdn $14.95 us